*Suddenly Chareen was lying
on the bed—fully dressed—
and Michael was on top of her.*

She gasped. His hard, warm body was pressed to hers in so many places. To have a man so close, so strong, was unbelievably intoxicating. It had been so long....

There was a moan starting deep in her throat. Was it a moan of surrender? Of triumph? Of overwhelming desire?

She would never know, because at that moment there was a new sound from the hallway: *"Mama? Mama?"*

Her eyes snapped open and she used the hands that had been kneading the muscles of his chest to throw him off her. She ran to the door and scooped into her arms the two little redheaded boys standing there.

"Where did *they* come from?" Michael asked.

Chareen looked at him, and her chin rose. "They're mine," she said proudly. "Say hello to Mr. Greco, boys. He's my boss."

Dear Reader,

We've been trying to capture what Silhouette Romance means to our readers, our authors and ourselves. In canvassing some authors, I've heard wonderful words about the characteristics of a Silhouette Romance novel—innate tenderness, lively, thoughtful, fun, emotional, hopeful, satisfying, warm, sparkling, genuine and affirming.

It pleases me immensely that our writers are proud of their line and their readers! And I hope you're equally delighted with their offerings. Be sure to drop a line or visit our Web site and let us know what we're doing right—and any particular favorite topics you want to revisit.

This month we have another fantastic lineup filled with variety and strong writing. We have a new continuity—HAVING THE BOSS'S BABY! Judy Christenberry's *When the Lights Went Out...* starts off the series about a powerful executive's discovery that one woman in his office is pregnant with his child. But who could it be? Next month Elizabeth Harbison continues the series with *A Pregnant Proposal*.

Other stories for this month include Stella Bagwell's conclusion to our MAITLAND MATERNITY spin-off. Go find *The Missing Maitland*. Raye Morgan's popular office novels continue with *Working Overtime*. And popular Intimate Moments author Beverly Bird delights us with an amusing tale about *Ten Ways To Win Her Man*.

Two more emotional titles round out the month. With her writing partner, Debrah Morris wrote nearly fifteen titles for Silhouette Books as Pepper Adams. Now she's on her own with *A Girl, a Guy and a Lullaby*. And Martha Shields's dramatic stories always move me. Her *Born To Be a Dad* opens with an unusual, powerful twist and continues to a highly satisfying ending!

Enjoy these stories, and keep in touch.

*Mary-Theresa Hussey*

Mary-Theresa Hussey,
Senior Editor

Please address questions and book requests to:
Silhouette Reader Service
U.S.: 3010 Walden Ave., P.O. Box 1325, Buffalo, NY 14269
Canadian: P.O. Box 609, Fort Erie, Ont. L2A 5X3

# Working Overtime

## RAYE MORGAN

SILHOUETTE *Romance*®

Published by Silhouette Books

America's Publisher of Contemporary Romance

To Kim Nadelson, for all those great editor things you do.

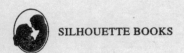 SILHOUETTE BOOKS

ISBN 0-373-19548-6

WORKING OVERTIME

Copyright © 2001 by Helen Conrad

Visit Silhouette at www.eHarlequin.com

**Printed in U.S.A.**

**Books by Raye Morgan**

Silhouette Romance

*Roses Never Fade* #427
*Promoted—to Wife!* #1451
*The Boss's Baby Mistake* #1499
*Working Overtime* #1548

Silhouette Desire

*Embers of the Sun* #52
*Summer Wind* #101
*Crystal Blue Horizon* #141
*A Lucky Streak* #393
*Husband for Hire* #434
*Too Many Babies* #543
*Ladies' Man* #562
*In a Marrying Mood* #623
*Baby Aboard* #673
*Almost a Bride* #717
*The Bachelor* #768
*Caution: Charm at Work* #807
*Yesterday's Outlaw* #836
*The Daddy Due Date* #843
*Babies on the Doorstep* #886
*Sorry, the Bride Has Escaped* #892
*\*Baby Dreams* #997
*\*A Gift for Baby* #1010
*\*Babies by the Busload* #1022
*\*Instant Dad* #1040
*Wife by Contract* #1100
*The Hand-Picked Bride* #1119
*Secret Dad* #1199

*The Baby Shower

## RAYE MORGAN

has spent almost two decades, while writing over fifty novels, searching for the answer to that elusive question: Just what is that special magic that happens when a man and a woman fall in love? Every time she thinks she has the answer, a new wrinkle pops up, necessitating another book! Meanwhile, after living in Holland, Guam, Japan and Washington, D.C., she currently makes her home in Southern California with her husband and two of her four boys.

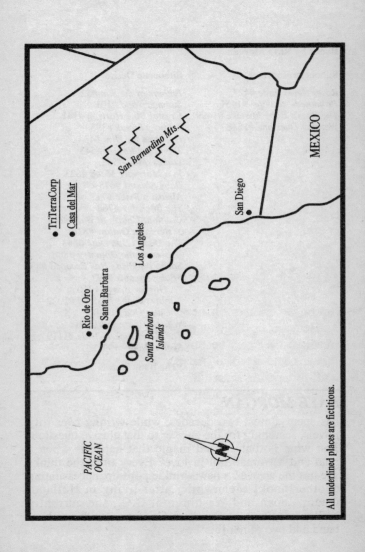

PACIFIC
OCEAN

Rio de Oro
Santa Barbara

*Santa Barbara
Islands*

Los Angeles

TriTerraCorp
Casa del Mar

*San Bernardino Mts.*

San Diego

MEXICO

N

All underlined places are fictitious.

# *Chapter One*

The first thing Michael Greco heard was her low, velvety voice, and when he heard it, the hair stood up on the back of his neck.

He froze, his hand on a volume of contract dispute records, his heart beating just a little faster. He'd never heard a voice like that before. It seemed to curl around his senses like a slinky cat might wrap itself around your ankles, all sleek and seductive, and at the same time, a provocative mystery that promised to stay just out of reach.

He'd come into the law section of TriTerraCorp's empty corporate library to do a little research over the lunch hour. For the last thirty minutes he'd been lost in his search, hidden by the tall bookcases, hardly noticing the group of women who'd come into the library after he'd arrived. The newcomers were gathered around the copy machine, laughing about something they seemed to be working on, obviously oblivious to the fact that he was in the room. The thick carpeting and the constant hum from the computers and other appliances helped to mask his presence. He'd ignored the women. But then that voice had arrived and greeted the others.

"Well, what do we have here?" she said, her voice husky in a way that stopped him in his tracks. "Is this a secret meeting of the Third Floor Conspiracy, or can anyone join in?"

"Hi, Char" came the slightly nervous answer, along with a rustling of paper. "We're just...uh... we're just..."

"Oh, let her see it," a higher voice said impatiently. "Char's okay. She won't turn us in. Look, Char, it's a calendar that we've been working on. Just something for laughs, to pass around the office."

"A calendar?" Her rich tone seemed to vibrate his senses. "How controversial can that be? Let's see it."

There was more rustling of paper.

"Oh, you naughty girls. What have you done?"

Her laugh was just as provocative as he'd thought it would be, and he narrowed his eyes, enjoying it.

"The Most Eligible Bachelors of TriTerraCorp. What a good idea. These pictures are priceless."

"Aren't they great? The office hunks. Sherry did

the graphics on her computer. She's an artist at this stuff.''

Michael softly slid the book back into place on the shelf, cursing himself for his involuntary reaction. He still had goose bumps, and it was just a voice, after all. The woman probably looked like a tree gnome.

And, anyway, it didn't matter if she did or she didn't. He'd promised himself a woman-free trip this time. He'd spent too much time dating interchangeable lovelies ever since his marriage had crumbled into the dust and left him grasping for a new focus to his life. Wine, women and song were never the answer to that problem—though it sometimes took a while to get that through thick heads like his.

''Ignore the voice,'' he muttered softly to himself, frowning as he tried to remember what he was looking for on the bookshelf.

But there it was again.

''You've even got Greg Holstein,'' she was recounting. ''He looks so cute in that lion suit! And Andy Martinez from Security as a trapeze artist. Sherry, this is a hoot.''

He swallowed hard. This was really strange. Her voice did something to him. It was almost the way a tuning fork resonated as it caught a note. He felt something respond inside every time she spoke. There was no use trying to pretend it wasn't happening. But nothing like this had ever happened to him before.

Maybe it was lack of sleep, he told himself grimly. After all, the night before he'd had a rough time. After a long, tiring flight from Florida, the company had put him up at the best hotel in Rio de Oro, but there was a rodeo in town filling most of the rooms and the partying had gone on fast and furious all night long. If he'd had a full hour's sleep, he hadn't noticed it, and now his eyes felt grainy and his head was throbbing. That had to be it. Fatigue had thrown off his internal balance or something.

Still, this had gone so far, he knew he had to see what this Char woman looked like. He tried to get a glimpse through the shelves, but the copy machine was at an angle and he only got a quick look at a flash of skirt. He was going to have to come out from the stacks and reveal himself if he wanted to see any more.

He sauntered casually out from behind the bookcase, and he could see the group of women clearly now. There were four of them, but the only one that held his gaze was the blonde who had her back to him. Her moonlight-silver hair was straight and silky as it fell halfway down to the small of her back. She wore a light blue suit that was cut snuggly enough to reveal a trim, firm body with a neat waist and hips that were appealingly round and inviting. There was a slit in the skirt that showed off legs as long as any he'd ever seen. If this was a tree gnome, they were making them less gnomelike these days.

"And…oh wait," she was saying, pulling out a new page that hadn't been attached to the others yet just as he settled his attention on her. "Is this Michael Greco person the new acquisitions specialist who's supposed to arrive today? How did you get a picture of him so quickly? I thought he'd just been loaned out by the Miami office. Is he even here yet?"

At that moment, one of the women turned her head and noticed him and her mouth dropped open in horror.

"He's here," the tall blonde named Sherry was saying. "I saw him when he checked in this morning and I didn't have to think twice. Listen, one look at the boy and you know he's calendar material. I snuck that photo from Human Resources. That's what we were working on when you came in, making copies. I've got to get the original back before lunch hour is over."

Another of the women noticed Michael and began tugging on the arm of the third. But so far, Char didn't know he was there, and Sherry didn't, either.

"The funny thing is, I've just been assigned to do some research for him," Char said musingly, holding the calendar out as though to get a better perspective. "Hmm…." Her voice trailed off.

"Isn't he a cutie?" Sherry asked, beaming.

"A cutie? I don't know." Char put her head to the side as though she couldn't quite get a fix on the picture. "He's got that playboy look in his eyes, if you ask me."

Sherry's head swung around and she blanched. By now all three women knew Michael was standing just a few feet away. Only Char was oblivious.

"Uh...Char?" Sherry whispered urgently.

But Char was lost in contemplating the picture in the calendar.

"I'll go even further," she said. "I'd say he's got a shifty look. His eyes are too close together. And there's a ruthless set to his mouth I don't really go for." She shook her head. "Nope. I don't like him."

"Char!" Sherry wailed, reaching out as though to grab her friend and run.

But Michael didn't give her time to do that. Stepping forward, he put a hand on the blonde's shoulder.

"A real shady character, huh?" he drawled. "Here, let me have a look."

Char slapped the calendar to her chest, spun on her heels and stared up into his hazel eyes. Her own eyes widened, then she blinked.

"Oops," she said, making a face.

He looked down into her sparkling gaze and forgot to breathe for a moment. Yes, the face was just as good as the rest of her. That hair the color of moonbeams framed skin as pale as fine china with eyes as blue as a summer sky. Her lips were full and lush and perfect for kissing, and when he finally did draw in a breath, her wildflower-fresh scent filled his head. He felt a surge of desire so strong, a part of him wanted to grab her and carry her off to some private place, caveman-style. If there had ever been such a thing as a woman made especially for him, this would have been her.

He swallowed hard and forced himself to ignore that fact. "May I see the picture?" he asked coolly, holding out his hand.

She shook her head, holding the calendar tightly to her chest. "Oh, no, Mr. Greco, I don't think you want to do that," she warned, her eyes full of apprehension.

The other women were murmuring a warning as well, but he didn't pay any attention. "Come on," he said, his gaze holding Chareen's. "How bad can it be?"

A flash of resentment flared in her gaze and he wondered if he'd come off a bit too arrogant. That was just as well, of course. He'd vowed to keep his distance from all attractive women on this trip, so why not lay a firm foundation? Still, he smiled as he held out his hand again.

She hesitated, then slowly pulled the calendar away from her body and handed it to him.

He looked down and frowned. "What the hell…?" he said, looking up at her and then down at the calendar again.

The picture had his head right, but the rest was pure fantasy. Somehow Sherry had attached the head from his file picture to the body of an extremely muscular pirate, ruffled shirt open to his waist, pants that fit like leotards and revealed more than was prudent. A jaunty black eye patch and a curved sword completed the picture. All in all, the result looked closer to a male stripper than it did to anything resembling reality. He looked into Chareen's eyes again. Was that laughter he saw playing hide-and-seek among the silvery shimmers?

"It's just a joke," she said quickly. "They don't mean anything by it."

"It's all in fun, Mr. Greco," Sherry chimed in, snatching the calendar from him with a nervous smile and beginning to back from the room. "I'm sorry if you're offended. I'll take your picture out. I'll tear it up." She demonstrated, ripping it out of the calendar and tearing it right before his eyes. "I'll burn it. No one will ever see it again. I swear." With a wide-eyed look at Chareen, she turned and disappeared through the doorway, along with her two co-conspirators. Giggling could be heard in the halls, then silence.

Chareen cleared her throat and tried to look innocent. Holding out her hand, she looked up at him and smiled brightly. "Well, Mr. Greco. It's nice to meet you. I'm Chareen Wolf. I guess we'll be working together for a few weeks."

Or...maybe not. He hesitated before taking her hand. There was no hint of amusement in his gaze, and she wondered for just a moment if he was going to hold what he'd heard her say against her. Should she apologize? Or pretend to have forgotten all about it?

But he finally did accept her handshake, though his side of it was rather perfunctory. "You are the expert in old Spanish land grants, aren't you?" he said crisply, his eyes cool as they assessed her. "I was told I was going to need you if I wanted to get the acquisitions accomplished in a timely manner."

"Guilty as charged," she admitted, refusing to let him see any nervousness on her part. "I'm a paralegal. I know something about early-nineteenth-century Spanish legal language. And I specialize in researching old deeds."

He nodded. "Just what I'm going to need." He gestured toward the doorway. "Why don't we stop in at the coffee shop and work up our strategy for this project over a cup of coffee?"

She hesitated. She'd had other plans for the rest of her lunch hour. But she supposed they could wait. For the time being, he was the boss. "Fine," she said, turning toward the doorway.

They didn't speak again as they strode side by side down the hallway. Chareen stared straight ahead, but her mind was racing. She wasn't sure she could do this. Michael Greco was nothing like what she'd expected.

The last acquisitions specialist she'd worked with had been a huge, balding man with a laugh that shook the rafters of the building. They had worked really well together, and when she'd told Leonard

Trask, the Legal Services manager who was almost like a second father to her, that she would be willing to take that sort of assignment again, she had expected to be paired with another older, nonthreatening sort of man. But Sherry had been right about one thing. Michael Greco belonged in a hunk calendar.

That in itself wasn't going to be easy to deal with. It had been a long, long time since she'd had a man in her life, and she was determined it would be a much longer time before anything like that happened again. She had two little boys at home who were the result of her last experiment in romance. Her life was set. She was a single mom, and she had no intention of being anything else for the time being. Working closely with a man who had this sort of masculine appeal was not going to be a piece of cake.

But there was more. There was something about him that bothered her to the core of her soul and made her wish she could think of a way to get out of this assignment. She'd noticed it from the first, when she'd seen the picture Sherry had made from the photo she'd borrowed from Human Resources. He reminded her of someone—Danny McGuire, the father of those two little boys. It was just a fluke, of course, just a chance resemblance. But it was enough to make her wish she was anywhere but here. She only hoped they could get on with the business at hand and get it over with. The sooner the better.

She chose a latte, while Michael Greco poured himself a large cup of some very black blend, and they made their way to a table near the window, overlooking the rolling green lawn that led down to a small, reed-fringed duck pond. He made a move as though thinking of pulling her chair out for her, but she hurriedly pulled it out for herself, then felt a bit foolish for having done so.

But what the heck? She'd been doing things that made her look foolish from the very beginning with this man. She wasn't sure why that bothered her so much, but it did. And that was unusual, because she was known around here for being a little sassy, a little brash, and a whole lot sure of herself. It wasn't true, of course. But she had managed to develop the reputation. It was a good shield against her real feelings.

She glanced at him sideways as he began to talk, going over the fundamentals of the White Stones project. Did he really look a lot like Danny, or was she imagining things? He did have the same sort of thick brown hair, cut very much like Danny used to wear it. And his hazel eyes were just as knowing. But his nose was straighter. His had more of a Roman look, whereas Danny's had looked as though it had been molded by a street fight or two. And his mouth was different. Danny's had always been twisted in a mocking grin. Michael Greco had only smiled once that she knew of, when they had first come face-to-face. Ever since, she'd been getting the feeling that he didn't want to be with her any more than she wanted to be with him. She moved restlessly in her seat, wondering why this meeting was so uncomfortable for them both. Maybe, for some people, it was dislike at first sight.

She wished, suddenly, that she was with her children. Three-year-old twins, they were at a stage where they were alternately adorable and infuriating, and she hated missing even a minute of their development. This had been a particularly topsy-turvy week, because she'd had to move her little family out of their home, as the landlord was doing some long-overdue repairs and painting. For the time being, they were living in quarters made available to TriTerraCorp employees, and the boys were having a little trouble getting used to it. Half of her mind was going over ideas of things she could do to make it up to her children, while the other half was listening to her new temporary boss.

"Don't you agree?" he asked her suddenly.

Startled, she looked up and met his steely gaze. She had no idea what he'd asked her to agree to. He'd made her feel foolish again, and he'd done it on purpose. Her chin rose. "I never contradict the boss," she said crisply, giving him a look of pure challenge.

His nod seemed to acknowledge that she'd gotten out of that one pretty well. Just as she settled back, pleased with herself, someone opened a door to the terrace and a sudden breeze swept through the room, scattering cups and papers. A napkin rose from the center of their table and Chareen reached to catch it. Michael reached for it at the same time, and somehow their hands met, fingers tangling. Electricity sizzled through her system and her gaze met his. The heat was sizzling through him, too. She could see the evidence in his eyes.

They both drew back as though they'd been burned and he quickly began talking again, going over the land that had been earmarked for the White Stones purchase, the various long-range uses of the property, the potential for the master-planned resort that was in the works. But her pulse was racing. She stared down at her latte and wondered if she was going crazy.

Michael went on, going over the fine points of the project and detailing the problems they were having with the Coastal Commission, which oversaw environmental concerns, but she was already familiar with most of what he was telling her, and her mind was wandering again. She knew from experience that this work would take a few months, at least.

Months, working side by side with this man. How often would their hands touch? How often would his gaze catch hers and kindle that shivery feeling? She didn't want to think about it.

But there was no way she could get out of this, short of quitting her job. She was the only one who had the background to research the old Spanish land grants. He couldn't do this without her. But somehow she was going to have to find a way to keep their actual physical contact to a minimum.

"We're set to include two golf courses," he was saying. "A convention center and a main hotel, along with two subsidiary hotels, one more of a spa and the other a sort of bed-and-breakfast. Then there will be a tract of condominiums, and a small, up-scale shopping area, including four restaurants."

Deciding that she'd better get with the program, she made an appropriate comment. "Wow. How large is the projected property?"

"About eight hundred acres. Mostly along a canyon that opens onto a wide beach."

She frowned. That sounded familiar. "Where exactly is it?"

"North of Gaviota, south of Vandenberg Air Force Base."

She nodded. That was a beautiful area of Southern California and she was looking forward to working there. She had an elderly uncle who still lived in the area. She'd visited his rickety beach house often as a child, walking down to the ocean on hot summer days. It was going to be fun being back there. But she was going to have to be wary.

A friend of hers had a saying she was always repeating, "If you don't want to get burned, stay away from the fire." Words of wisdom. She was going to keep them in mind.

* * *

Michael checked his watch and stifled a groan. They'd only been sitting here for a little over a quarter of an hour. It felt like much longer. The obnoxious minutes were dragging their scruffy little feet. This was like some type of unbearable medieval torture.

He glanced over at Chareen. She was staring down into her drink and he took the opportunity to take a good look at her.

He took in her silky curtain of hair, the soft curve of her cheek, her elegant chin line, and then his gaze trailed down into the opening of her blouse, where the upper swell of her breasts was barely visible. Reaction surged through him and he had to look away quickly, grabbing his coffee cup and draining it in one long swallow. It was as though someone had picked up one of his teenage dreams, looked inside and pulled out everything he liked in a woman, then mixed it all together and presented him with Chareen Wolf. There wasn't a flaw on her. She was the sort of female who made grown men think about chucking it all and heading to the South Seas in a sailboat with only her on board.

His mind slipped back to a picture of Grace, his ex-wife. She'd been just as pretty, but every time he thought of her now, all he saw was the haunting look of disappointment in her eyes. It had been four years since he'd seen her, but the memory of that look still had the power to make him bleed.

So he'd spent the last few years looking for love in all the wrong places—on purpose. No commitments, no promises, no more disappointed looks. Casual relationships were all he could handle. He'd thought he was beyond being easily aroused any longer. That is, until he'd heard Chareen Wolf's voice in the library.

But that wasn't what he'd come to California for and he couldn't let himself get sidetracked. The TriTerraCorp CEO had taken him to lunch before he'd left Florida and made it very clear that there was a vice presidency riding on this job in California. That would be great. After all, wasn't that what he had been working toward for the last few years?

Business, Not Pleasure. That was going to be his motto on this project. He'd promised himself as much, and he knew he had the self-discipline to keep that promise. But working side by side with Chareen Wolf was not going to make it any easier.

But wait a minute. Here was a thought. Why did they have to work together side by side? After all, he was the executive officer here. He set strategy, others implemented his orders. He could set it up in any way he chose, and a good way was beginning to form in his mind right now.

He glanced at Chareen. "You know," he told her casually, "I understand that you are used to working without too much direct supervision. Your department head told me you are the best TriTerraCorp has got at this sort of thing."

She gazed at him brightly. "Well, I think I'm pretty good at my job," she admitted.

He smiled at her. "So I hear. And I'm sure you'd prefer to work without me breathing down your neck all the time. So how about this?" He leaned forward, giving her a direct look that seemed to startle her. "Why don't you set up your own schedule and make your reports to me through Leonard Trask, your supervisor. That way, you'll have complete autonomy, unless I find any problem with your work. Though I hardly expect to do that."

She sat up a bit straighter and seemed excited. "That's a great idea," she told him. "So, in other words, I'll reserve time at city hall to delve into the archives and go over the deeds, then set up my own interviews with sources, write up a report and hand it to Leonard, who will pass it on to you."

"Exactly." He was pleased to see she was as quick as he'd heard she was. But just a little surprised that she seemed as eager for this hands-off approach as he was. When you came right down to it, he wasn't used to women finding excuses to avoid his company. But that was neither here nor there. "You'll still be available for any follow-ups we might need, of course."

"I love it," she said, smiling from ear to ear, her eyes shining. "Mr. Greco, you're going to spoil me."

"Believe me, Ms. Wolf, you're doing me a favor."

Great. She was going for it. He stretched back in his chair and risked a smile. He was a genius.

"That," he told himself silently, "is why they pay you the big bucks, Greco. You are the man with the plan."

# *Chapter Two*

Chareen shed her clothes with a sigh of relief and stepped into the shower as though it were a waterfall on a tropical mountainside. The water felt so good running through her hair and down over her skin, and it had been such a long day.

She'd picked up her two little ones, Ricky and Ronnie, at the day-care center and had driven them directly to their favorite fast-food restaurant for hamburgers. She'd then spent an hour trying to ward off constantly impending disaster as they charged through the room with the plastic balls and sailed down the long tube slide and climbed anything with a handhold. There was a lot of noise involved—and an apology to the man who was hit in the head with one of the plastic balls when her two wild ones had a ball war. And then there was the little girl who started crying because Ronnie made a face at her. But finally she'd been able to convince the boys to get back in the car and she'd dragged them back here to Casa del Mar, the old Victorian house where they were staying.

A sort of corporate bed-and-breakfast, the three-floor structure had been renovated to provide rooms for contract workers and other temporary visitors to TriTerraCorp. When she'd told Leonard, her supervisor, about having to find a place to stay while her house was being repaired, he'd suggested she stay there for the duration. Currently half empty, the house had plenty of room for her and her two boys.

"Just keep those kids quiet," Leonard had warned her. "Some of the old-timers who stay at Casa del Mar are real cranky when it comes to the sound of kids."

Keeping Ricky and Ronnie quiet would require depriving them of the power of speech, and even then they would surely pound on drums to get their message out. But she did her best, hurrying them in through the lobby area and up the stairs to the room on the second floor where they were staying. She bathed them, read them a story and put them to bed. At last, she had a few minutes to unwind.

And to think about what had happened at work. She'd been putting off thinking about it, because there were just too many ramifications to deal with all at once. Michael Greco had rocked her world, whether he knew it or not. She only hoped he didn't know it.

And it wasn't just that he looked so much like Danny. At least, she thought he did. She wished she'd brought a picture along when they'd moved in here so that she could get it out and take a look and see if this was all in her imagination. Funny how blurry his image was to her now. There had been a time when she'd been so in love with that face, she thought she'd die if she couldn't be with him.

Well, she hadn't been with him for a very long time now, and she was still very much alive—though it had been touch-and-go for a while there. Everyone had always warned her that Danny would disappear from her life. No one had expected it to happen quite the way it had, though, in a fiery car accident that took his life. And no one had known she would have two little red-headed boys to remind her of the love she'd had for too short a time.

She'd had three years to get over it, and she'd done a pretty good job. Her life was full of her kids, and her job, in that order. There was no room for anything or anyone else. Especially not a man who stirred up painful memories—and her long-dormant sensual imagination.

Slipping out of the shower, she dried herself with one of the big, fluffy towels that Hannah Schubert, the house manager, had stocked in the bathroom, then stepped into the bottoms of her Mickey Mouse shorty pajamas and pulled on the top. She twisted her hair into a clip at the back, slipped her feet into fluffy pink bedroom slippers and made a face as she caught sight of herself in the mirror. This was not a picture she would want anyone she knew to ever see.

Stopping to peek in on her sleeping babies, she paused and smiled, her heart full as she looked at them. Those adorable little angelic faces. Who could guess that all they were doing was storing up the energy to drive everyone crazy again as soon as possible?

She grinned and turned to go downstairs. Her stomach was grumbling. She'd been too busy to eat at the fast-food restaurant and a peanut butter sandwich would hit the spot right now.

She moved through the hallway with the confidence born of the knowledge that she was the only one home. Besides herself and her little family, four other people were living in the house right now. Hannah was the house mother and all-around coordinator of most of what went on here. And then there were two contract workers from Seattle who were busy improving the accounting software used by Financial, and an engineer from the Dallas office who was consulting on a sports stadium project. Hannah had gathered them all together to go out to the arena to see an all-star roster of country singers entertain, part of the rodeo that was in town. Chareen had been tempted, but she'd turned down the opportunity for a little fun. It was much more important to her to spend what time she could with her children.

She padded into the kitchen and looked around the room, enjoying the contrast to her own little tiny kitchen at home. The stove was a huge gleaming monstrosity, the refrigerator had three doors, side by side, the sink had all the latest attachments, and beautiful copper-bottomed pans hung over the center island. Think of the gourmet dinners she could concoct in this place. Sighing happily, she switched on the radio and reached into the bread box. A cha-cha came on the air and she began to sing along with it, adding a few dance steps with her pink-slippered feet at the same time.

Now where did Hannah keep the peanut butter?

Michael paused on the wooden steps and looked up at the beautiful old house. He was feeling better already. He needed sleep and he needed it soon. This looked like a place where he might be able to get it.

He knocked on the big wooden door with the beveled glass windowpanes, but there was no answer. In the distance, he could hear a radio playing, and the sound of someone singing. Trying the knob, he found it turned easily in his hand, and he went on into the entryway.

The place looked just as good inside as out. Polished hardwood floors gleamed in the lamplight. Persian carpets, neoclassic furniture, reproductions of works by Constable and Turner, and plenty of flower arrangements all combined to lend the place an air of quiet dignity and peaceful serenity. And most of all, after the wild scene at the hotel where rodeo rowdies caroused through the corridors all night long, there was the wonderful silence that lurked in the hallways.

Sighing happily, he set his leather suitcase and canvas suit carrier on the floor of the entryway and started toward where the radio was playing. He'd been told to ask for a Hannah Schubert, who managed the place. In just minutes, he was sure his head would be on a cool, crisp pillow. He could hardly wait.

Pushing open the swinging door to the kitchen, his gaze encountered a woman in baby doll pajamas and fluffy pink slippers, hair only half caught in a band at the back of her head. She was just taking a huge bite out of a peanut butter sandwich and catching sight of him at the same time.

"You're not Hannah Schubert, are you?" he asked wryly, knowing the answer before the words were out of his mouth. For some reason, finding Chareen here didn't really surprise him. After all, he'd been thinking about her all afternoon.

But Chareen seemed surprised. She gasped, breathed the wrong way and began to choke on the peanut butter. He was at her side in two quick strides, pulling her into the curl of one arm while he pounded on her back with the flat of his free hand.

Funny. For such a slim thing, she felt solid and deliciously rounded against his arm. He wanted to keep her there for a while, but she was already fighting to get free of him and he let her go reluctantly.

"You!" she cried as she backed away, still coughing, her face red and her eyes watering. She couldn't believe it. Was she cursed or something? There he stood, big as life, looking incredibly handsome with his hair mussed so that it fell over his forehead, his tie hanging loose and the top button of his shirt undone. He was so masculine and attractive, it made her ache inside. What had she done to deserve this?

"It must be kismet," he was saying dryly, looking at her with a bemused smile. "We meet again."

She would have kept on backing right out of sight if she could have, but the counter stopped her. Still staring at him, ready to jump should he make a move toward her, she licked the peanut butter from her fingers and reached for a paper towel to finish the job.

"What are you doing here?" she demanded, embarrassed to be caught running around in her pajamas, intrigued by the sight of him and chagrined to think he might realize just how much she liked what she saw.

"What are *you* doing here?" he countered, looking her up and down and knowing he was being blatant about it, but unable to resist. She looked good enough to kiss, even in her present disheveled condition, and he realized he wasn't as displeased as he should have been to find her thrust back into his day.

"I have permission to stay here," she told him, drawing herself up rather grandly for a person who'd just been choking to death on peanut butter in his embrace. She pulled her arms across her chest in a defiant posture, meant to outweigh the picture she knew she made in her childish pajamas. "My house is being repaired and I needed a place to stay for a few days, so Leonard, my supervisor, suggested I stay here."

"What a coincidence," he told her, amusement sparkling in his eyes. "I have special permission to stay here, too."

She frowned. That was all she needed. Surely he was mistaken. "No," she said sternly. "You can't stay here. This place is for contract workers and visitors from other branches of TriTerraCorp. You're an executive. Executives stay at the hotel. The company has a very expensive suite for them." She gestured with a jerk of her head. "You'll have to go and stay there."

"I've been," he told her tranquilly. "And I left again. There's a rodeo, you know."

She blinked, thinking that over. "I know. But it's not at the hotel."

"It may not be, but the cowboys are. They're riding the place hard and they plan to die with their boots on. I didn't get any sleep at all last night. Tonight, I plan to sleep like a baby."

Her shoulders drooped. She knew she'd probably lost this one. It was so annoying to see him standing there so easily, as though he belonged, telling her the way things were going to be. She wished with all her heart that she could honestly tell him there was just no vacancy. But the way things were going, he'd probably find a way to have *her* kicked out and take over her room.

"Okay," she told him grudgingly, "but if you're going to be staying here, you've got to promise me one thing."

"What's that?"

"Promise that you won't keep sneaking up on me like this. I'm going to be jumpy as a cat for as long as you're around."

He grinned. He couldn't help it. She was just so damn appealing. "I promise."

"Good." She heaved a sigh, as though that took a real load off her mind. "Okay, here are the rules. We're all equal here. No bosses. No ordering anyone around. Everyone gets a bedroom, but we all share one bathroom on each floor. There's a 'knock three times and pause' rule on all the doors, especially the bathroom door, because the locks are old and cranky. Sometimes they don't work very well."

She paused, waiting to see if that was enough to scare him away. When it obviously wasn't, she sighed and went on. "You're supposed to supply some of your own food, though Hannah keeps a stock of staples that everyone is welcome to use. She has them clearly marked. She makes breakfast available for all from six to seven-thirty every morning.''

He nodded, agreeing to the rules as she'd stated them. "That all sounds very good." He flexed his shoulders. He would have liked to stay here chatting with her for hours. That husky voice of hers still worked its magic on his senses, and he had to admit, she was a hit in those diminutive pajamas. It just about made a man forget all about some ridiculous promises he'd made to himself.

She was acting skittish, but something told him she might be receptive with the right persuasion. Why not give it a try? A knowing smile, a touch, a raised eyebrow—he knew the ropes. He might even get her to share a bed with him this very night.

But, much as he was tempted, he knew he wasn't going to do it. She wasn't a player. She had all the earmarks of a woman who viewed marriage and family as a major goal, and that was the very kind of woman he avoided at all costs.

Besides, he was dead tired. He had to get some sleep. After one last regretful look at how cute her breasts looked under that ridiculous pajama top, he sighed and asked, "How do I find out which room I've got?"

She shrugged. "You'll have to ask Hannah. She and everyone else in the place are at the rodeo.

They'll be back about midnight, I'm sure. Now, if you'll just hand me the other half of my sandwich,'' she added, pointing out where it lay on the counter behind him, ''I'm going to bed.''

He picked up her sandwich but he didn't hand it to her right away. ''Midnight,'' he said, frowning. ''No, that's impossible. I need a bed now.''

''Sorry,'' she said, stepping closer to take her sandwich and turning as though about to flee.

''Sorry' won't help,'' he said, grasping her wrist before she could pull away. ''I've got to get some sleep. Now.''

She glared up at him. ''What do you expect me to do about it?''

He raised an eyebrow. ''Oh, I don't know. Be a little helpful, maybe.''

Their gazes held a moment too long. That sense of awareness sizzled between them, and her heart was beating so loudly, she knew he had to hear it.

This was utterly ridiculous. How could she be standing here in these silly pajamas, with his hand holding her wrist in a viselike grip, feeling like a teenager with her first crush? Determinedly, she yanked her hand away and glared at him, rubbing her wrist.

But he hardly seemed to notice. ''What rooms are empty?'' he asked crisply.

''I don't know,'' she said, knowing she was acting like a sullen child but unable to help herself. ''I don't pay much attention.''

"Don't you?" His gaze narrowed. "What floor are you on?"

"The second. But..."

"Are there any empty rooms near you?"

"That's not the point."

"There must be a room across the hall from you. Anyone in there?"

She hesitated. "Not that I know of, but that doesn't mean..."

He started for the door. "It means I'm going to be sleeping there tonight."

"You can't," she said, hurrying after him back to the entryway.

"Oh, can't I?" He slung his suit carrier over his shoulder and picked up his suitcase, then turned to look at her. "Just watch me." He gestured for her to lead the way. "After you, fair lady."

She searched his eyes suspiciously, looking for any sign that he was making fun of her, but she couldn't pin anything down.

"Why can't you just camp out on the couch until they get back?" she suggested rather halfheartedly. She knew he wouldn't go for it and he didn't even bother to say so. Instead he waited, giving her a look of expectation, and she sighed and flounced off toward the stairs.

"The door might be locked," she said over her shoulder as he followed her to the second floor. "The bed might not be made up."

"I'll sleep in the bathtub if I have to," he said

calmly, not even pretending he didn't like the view he had in front of him going up the stairs. "Just give me a pillow and don't turn on the shower. Once I fall asleep, I don't plan to wake up again until morning."

She hurried to put distance between them, but stopped in front of the room she was staying in.

"Here's mine," she said, cracking open the door to deposit the peanut butter sandwich just inside and to sneak a peek at her sleeping boys. They looked fine, and she closed the door again just as he arrived.

"And here's the room you plan to hijack," she said, trying the handle. It opened easily. She went straight to the bed and pulled back the bedspread. "I thought so. No sheets."

"I'll rough it."

"No, you won't." She was scandalized. "I'll find you sheets. Here, help me pull back the blanket. I'll make your bed up for you. Just wait a minute."

He pulled back the blanket as she'd suggested, then shrugged out of his jacket, pulled off his tie and began unbuttoning his shirt. All he wanted to do was fall down on the bed and close his eyes, but he waited while she opened drawers, looking for bedding.

Her hair had come completely loose by now, and it swirled around her pretty face in a way that made him want to kiss her nose. She looked so beguiling with the tanned skin of her long legs gleaming in the lamplight. But when she'd found the sheets and turned, coming back toward him, he had to laugh at the picture she made. Her legs were lovely, but it did look as though she were wearing two very angry Persian cats on her feet.

"What?" she said indignantly, stopping in her tracks. "What's so funny?"

"Nothing," he said quickly, shrugging out of his shirt and dropping it onto a nearby chair. "Nothing at all."

She was going to say more, but one look at his muscular chest rendered her speechless and she looked away quickly, praying that she wouldn't turn red as she moved toward the bed with the fresh sheets. The picture Sherry had created in the calendar had nothing on the reality. It had been a long time since she'd been this close to a real live shirtless man. She wondered, fleetingly, if he would notice if she turned up the air conditioner. It seemed to be getting awfully hot in the room.

"Here, grab this side," she ordered as she tossed the sheets down and began to pull the fitted one into place.

He did as he'd been told and they got the sheet on in no time. Chareen reached for the top one and gave it a swish, looked up and caught Michael's eye as he grabbed his side, and her heart did a flip in her chest. There was something in the way he was looking at her...

"Pull it tight," she ordered, avoiding his gaze and

trying to keep her equilibrium. Just a few more minutes and she would be out of here.

"Yes, ma'am," he said, his voice like a purr.

"Tuck it under, like this," she said, demonstrating a hospital corner.

He gazed at her balefully. "What is the point?" he asked, making no effort to attempt one.

With an exasperated sigh, she charged around the end of the bed to do it herself, but he didn't make way fast enough, and when he did move, it was in the wrong direction. She turned right into him, their bodies collided, and the next thing she knew, she was falling down onto the bed, and he was falling on top of her. She gasped. He broke his fall with his arms, bracing himself over her, looking down into her face.

"Sorry," he said, but he didn't move.

She knew she should say something, but she seemed to have lost all power of speech. Her gaze was locked with his, and she felt as though she were lost, wandering in the shadows of his hazel eyes, unable to find a way out. His hard, warm body was pressed to hers in so many places. To have a man so close, so strong, was unbelievably intoxicating. It had been so long since a man had held her in his arms and made sweet love to her.

Suddenly, she ached to have that feeling again. Her senses drank in every nuance of his presence, his clean, manly scent, the brush of his breath against her hair, the hard muscles of his thighs pressing on hers. Her hands were flattened against his naked chest, and she could feel his heart beating a pulse into her palm.

"I hold your heart in my hand." The sentiment flickered through her mind and for one very scary moment, she was afraid she might have said it out loud.

But there wasn't time to worry about that, because her body was turning traitor. A shudder ran through her soul and she knew she wanted him in a strange, deep and very primitive way. The need had an urgency that took her breath away and seemed about to convulse her body, as though she'd been taken over by a libidinous spirit that would soon render her helpless to resist. Her lips parted and she found herself arching toward him, begging for his kiss. There was a moan starting deep in her throat. Was it a moan of surrender? Of triumph? Of overwhelming desire?

She would never know, because at that moment there was a new sound from the hallway.

"Mama? Mama?"

As though a switch had been thrown, her eyes snapped wide and she used those hands that had been kneading into the muscles of his chest to throw him off her. Springing to her feet, she called out, "Just a minute, baby," and glared at where Michael was sprawled on the bed, looking as though he wasn't sure what had just happened here.

"If you need anything else, Mr. Greco," she said

evenly, "you can wait for Hannah to get back. I'm off duty. See you in the morning."

She stared at him for a short moment, as though she could hardly believe what they'd just shared could have really happened, then she spun around, threw open the door and headed into the hallway.

He rose slowly from the bed, still throbbing deep down with the need for her. His mind was fogged with exhaustion and desire, and he really wasn't sure what was going on. Reaching the doorway, he leaned against the jamb and looked out into the hallway, watching as she scooped two little redheaded boys into her arms.

"Where did they come from?" he asked, completely at sea and mainly intent on getting her to come back into the room.

She looked up at him and her chin lifted. "They're mine," she said proudly. "Ricky and Ronnie. Say hello to Mr. Greco, boys. He's my boss."

# Chapter Three

Michael groaned softly.

Char was not going to be coming back in the bedroom. Not only that, but he now had ample evidence that his first impression had been the right one. She wasn't the type to be interested in a quick roll in the hay. Especially not with two kids in tow.

The boys both blinked at him sleepily. One boy waved. The other frowned and turned his head away, pressing into his mother's neck. Michael stared at them. He was not a kid person.

"You didn't tell me you had children," he said, resignation clear in his voice.

"You didn't ask." She turned into her room, looking back at him. His attitude had cooled completely and she wondered why. But she had two children to look after and she didn't have time to dwell on it.

"Good night," she called back over her shoulder.

He didn't answer, but she heard his door close as she put the boys back to bed. Frowning, she closed her own door and leaned against it for a moment, remembering what had happened on the bed. It was crazy, of course. She must have been half out of her mind. She didn't do things like that, not ever.

But she couldn't say that anymore, could she? She'd responded to him like a flower to sunshine, as though she'd been waiting for him to awaken something in her that had been sleeping too long. Was she really that lonely? Did her body and soul really hunger so deeply for a man's love that she was ready to drop down on a bed with the first guy who grabbed her?

Or was it something else? Was it because he looked so much like Danny? Was that what had loosened her inhibitions and made her respond to him the way she had?

"Hah!" she said to herself scornfully. No such luck. She couldn't claim that as an alibi. Her mind had been on nothing but the touch, the scent and the heat of Michael Greco. Which was why he was more dangerous to her peace of mind than any man she'd known in a long, long time.

"Mama, kiss!" Ronnie demanded from his bed, holding his little arms out to her.

Smiling, she started toward him, loving the way

his little fireplug body looked in his Pokémon pajamas.

"Forget about Michael Greco," she told herself sternly. "Your kids are all that really matter." And she wiped him from her mind as her children claimed her full attention.

Michael went to bed, but despite his exhaustion, he found himself lying still, staring at the ceiling. Maybe he was too tired to relax. Or maybe he was still trying to get over his encounter with his neighbor.

He could still feel the way her body had pressed against his. Every delicious part of her fulfilled the promise that rich, husky voice laid out. It had been a long time since a woman had turned him on quite so easily and quite so thoroughly. And here he'd thought he was finished with that sort of thing.

It had been four years since his wife, Grace, had given up on him. He'd had his share of women since then, and over time, the nameless, faceless encounters had begun to seem sleazy and pointless. He'd made a decision to forget about women and concentrate on business. He had ambitions. Right now he was on a trajectory toward a vice presidency. That should be enough. And it was, damn it!

He couldn't have a life like other men because he wasn't like other men. He accepted that. He could live with it. But it had been bad luck to end up so close to Chareen Wolf and her crew. Something in her had reached right through his defenses and latched onto his soul from the beginning. He hadn't wanted it to happen. But she reminded him of what life could have been like if only...

"If onlys" didn't change anything. He was a pragmatic man and reality was all he cared about. And reality dictated that he stay away from women like Char—women who had family in mind.

Poor Grace. Suddenly he had a clear picture of her, of that awful pleading look in her eyes. Even after all these years, that look made him shrivel up inside. All she'd ever wanted was a family. And that was exactly what he couldn't give her.

Char was nothing like Grace, but she had similar interests. He had to stay away from her. For his own sanity, for her peace of mind. And with that decided, he finally fell asleep.

Michael's eyes drifted open a crack. Sunlight spilled into his room. He glanced at the clock. Damn. He'd forgotten to set the alarm. He closed his eyes again. No use getting up until he was sure the coast was clear. Might as well get a little more sleep.

This was his third morning in the old Victorian. On the first and second he had very carefully awoken early and cleared out before Char and her children got up, getting breakfast at a local coffee shop and heading for work in time to avoid all contact with the little family across the hall. He'd had to deal with Char a few times at the office, but he'd managed to keep the contact short and sweet—and very reserved. Neither one of them had made any reference to the incident on the bed. Relations between them were strictly professional and they were going to stay that way if he could manage it.

But this morning he'd misjudged. He'd gotten in so late last night, he'd prepared for bed like a robot and fallen asleep instantly. Now he was going to have to spend some more time in his room if he was going to wait them out and emerge after they'd left the house. So he dozed, barely noticing as doors opened and closed up and down the hall, as little feet pattered past, as Char's heels made a staccato but muffled tattoo on the corridor carpet.

He had a short, seductive dream in which he reached out and touched Char's shoulder, his hand sliding in between two silky strands of her beautiful blond hair, and she turned, dressed in the cranberry-colored, scoop-necked wool sweater she'd worn to work the day before—a sweater that did for her form what a layer of powdered snow did to the Sierras—and he reached down into the scoop and...

He woke with a start, blinking in the light. Wow. Why did he always wake up right at the good part? Yawning, he turned on his side. And stared right into a bright little face with very sparkling blue eyes peering at him over the side of the bed.

"Aaaa!" he yelled, jerking back.

"Aiiiii!" the little boy yelled back, ducking down out of sight.

"What the hell?" Michael ground out, furious. "Get out of here, kid. How did you get in here?"

"Ronnie!" Char's voice sounded out in the hall-way. "Ronnie, where are you?"

Michael looked over at the edge of his bed. The bright blue eyes were peering over the side of the mattress at him again.

"You're Ronnie, aren't you?" he said.

The thatch of red hair bounced as the boy nodded.

Michael considered his options. He had on nothing but pajama bottoms and he didn't relish leaping from the bed in them in front of all and sundry. That made him something of a prisoner here. Which left him with only one thing to do.

"Ronnie?" Char's voice said again, closer this time.

"He's in here," Michael called out, going up on one elbow. "Come and get him."

He could sense her hesitating outside his door.

"What?" she called from just outside.

"Come on in. Obviously, the door isn't locked." That was probably another thing he'd forgotten to do, besides the alarm.

The door opened. Char's pretty face peered in, looking suspicious. Her gaze met his, then bounced off and swept around the room. "Ronnie?" she said.

Ronnie giggled and threw himself down to try to wiggle under the bed.

"Ronnie!" She flew into the room and grabbed a leg, pulling him back out. He chortled as she pulled him up into her arms, but she didn't look as though she thought this was a laughing matter herself.

"Ronnie!" she admonished him crossly. "Don't you ever go into strange rooms without asking first. You hear?"

Ronnie turned his head so that he could look at Michael. "I got a 'elphant,'" he told him brightly. "He goes 'whoo!'" He raised his face as he made the elephant call, then grinned from ear to ear.

But his mother ignored this piece of information, turning so that she was the one who could look Michael in the face. "Don't you lock your door?" she said to him accusingly.

It was a moment of mixed emotion for Michael. On the one hand, he was thoroughly annoyed at having a child sneak into his room. On the other, he couldn't help but enjoy the picture Char made with the morning sunbeams lighting her silver hair like a spotlight. She was wearing a suit this morning, and the skirt was nice and short, showing off the sort of legs that could make a grown man tremble with longing. A woman interested in family and kids was poison as far as he was concerned, and he wasn't going to waver on that point. But just as a feast for the eyes, Char had it all. And he wasn't going to deny himself the enjoyment of looking. Just looking.

But he answered her with just a touch of sarcasm,

to remind himself—and her—that they were not destined to be a friendly pair.

"You know," he said, gazing at her from beneath lowered lids, "I wasn't expecting an invasion. I'll be more careful in the future."

"Good for you," she muttered, throwing him a piercing glare and turning to march off, her child slung over her shoulder. Ronnie looked back as they left, and gave Michael a gap-toothed grin. The door closed with a crisp snap.

*Maybe I can actually put up with having kids around if the bargain includes a good look at a woman like Char every morning,* he thought as he rose and went to his closet for a robe so that he could make his way to the second-floor bathroom for a shower.

But he changed his mind soon enough. Back from the shower, he put on slacks and a white shirt and tie, and reached for his suit coat, which he'd draped across the chair by the door when he'd come in the night before. A bright green sucker fell to the floor. A nice sticky sucker. And it had left a trail of green goo all down the front of the suit coat.

Uttering a very obscene word in a soft but vicious tone, he headed for the sink in the bathroom. A few minutes later he was dressed in his other suit and sauntering into the breakfast room where Char and her children were lingering over morning coffee and cereal. He arrived just in time to hear Char scolding one son.

"Ricky, put down that fork. You do not use a fork to eat your cereal. You're dripping milk all over. Use your spoon."

Michael stopped in the doorway and surveyed the room. The large circular table had evidence that other diners had come and gone, but for now, only Char and her brood occupied the far end. A couple of slices of toast, a few splinters of bacon and the remnants of scrambled eggs sat in chafing dishes on a sideboard. Three sets of eyes turned toward him and stared.

"Here come the man, Mama!" Ronnie cried, face alight.

At the same time, his twin brother Ricky looked right through the newcomer, as though he wasn't even there.

Char didn't say a thing, but her gaze was plainly cool.

Michael nodded to them all, then walked over and held the sticky sucker out to Char. "I think this must be yours," he said accusingly.

Char recoiled, but Ronnie gasped. "My 'pop'!" he cried, and he began to kick his feet as he reached out for it.

"Oh, is it yours?" Michael said dryly, handing it to the boy. After all, he knew very well Ronnie had to be the one who'd left it in his room.

But Char cried out, "No, you can't give it to him like that." She grabbed it away from her son.

"Look. It's got fuzz all over it." She waved it at him accusingly. "What have you done to it?"

It took him a couple of beats to realize she was actually blaming him for the condition of the sucker. "What have *I* done to it?" He stared at her, outraged. How had she managed to make her child the aggrieved party here?

"You're a grown man, aren't you?" She favored him with a scathing look up and down before rising, marching into the adjoining kitchen and turning on the faucet to wash off the candy. "You should be able to handle carrying a lollipop around without getting lint all over it," she called back to him.

"That lint happens to be what is left of my suit coat," he told her. "The rest of it has dissolved into green goo."

She looked at him and started to say something, but Ricky chose that moment to stick the fork into his tongue. He let out a shriek and Char was immediately immersed in comforting him.

Michael looked at Ronnie. Ronnie grinned at him, but there was something in the mischievous glint in his eyes that made Michael think he knew more than he was saying.

His instinct had been to keep his distance from these children, and now his instincts had been vindicated. Turning on his heel, he grabbed his briefcase from where he'd left it in the hall and started for the front door.

"Oh, Mr. Greco!" Hannah Shubert, a short,

plump, gray-haired lady, was hurrying after him. "Oh, you can't go yet. You haven't eaten one meal here in three days. I'd like to make you a special omelet. Please come back to the breakfast room."

He turned and managed a pleasant smile. The woman seemed very earnest in her zeal to please, and he hated to discourage that sort of thing. "I'm sorry. I missed my alarm and slept late. I've got to get to the office."

She put a hand on his arm and gave him a motherly smile. "I'll forgive you this time," she said. "But promise me you'll let me make you something for breakfast tomorrow."

He hesitated, knowing he was going to regret this. "Well..."

"Please. Whatever you like best, that's what I'll prepare." She coaxed him with a sweet smile. "Come on. What do you like?"

"Well..." He swallowed, then let memory take over. "What I really like is fresh-squeezed orange juice and sausages and crisp hash browns and really fat pieces of French toast dripping with butter and maple syrup."

"Done," she said with satisfaction. "Tomorrow, then."

"Tomorrow," he agreed, then gave her a smile and turned to head out the door toward his rented car. When he got in tonight, he'd have to tell her he would need to eat very, very early. Breakfast with

Char's twins was not an option. Not if he wanted to stay sane, at any rate.

"Well, isn't that nice?" Hannah commented as she bustled around the table, picking up after some of the earlier diners. "Mr. Greco promised he'd let me fix him a good breakfast tomorrow."

"What a sweetheart," Char said in return, not bothering to hide the sarcasm. "If you're really nice, maybe he'll let you iron his shirts."

"Now, now, my dear," Hannah said reprovingly. "You shouldn't take that attitude. I swear, women today." She shook her head, but her face was still wreathed in good-natured happiness. "He is such a handsome one, isn't he? And I hear he is on the fast track to the top. Prime executive material."

Char nodded. "No doubt about it," she murmured as she wiped up Ronnie's latest milk spill.

"You could do worse than setting your sights on that one," Hannah counseled.

Char rolled her eyes, but she made sure she was turned away so that Hannah couldn't see her do it. The woman meant well. But the thought of "setting her sights" on Michael Greco was too grotesque to tolerate.

She was thoroughly annoyed with him now. She'd thought he was a bit touchy the first day when he'd arrived, but ever since, he'd only gotten worse. Life at work was a constant hide-and-seek game, trying to find where he'd gone to get away from her this time.

"It's all in your mind," Lena Harold, who'd been assigned as his temporary secretary and had always been a good friend, had told her. "He's bouncing all over the place because he needs to get input from so many departments. It has nothing to do with hating you." And she threw back her dark, sleek head and laughed at the entire concept, gold earrings jangling.

But Chareen hadn't laughed back. She knew a job of evasion when she ran smack into one.

"Ronnie?" she said, turning from her mop-up task to find only Ricky still with her in the breakfast room. "Where is that scamp?"

She found him out in the front room. He'd climbed up in the window seat and was watching through the glass as Michael drove away.

"The man is in the car," he informed his mother as she scooped him up and carried him back to the breakfast room. "There he goes!"

"And we're going, too," she told him cheerfully, hugging him close. "As soon as we clean up and get our sweaters on." But her heart was breaking for her baby. It was becoming more and more obvious that he was fascinated with Michael's every move. But all the fascination in the world wasn't going to get him anywhere with that man.

She knew both of her boys were starved for adult male attention in their lives. They desperately needed a real man they could look up to and pattern their behavior on. But real men, like cowboys, were hard to find these days. And Michael Greco had made it quite clear that he wasn't going to put himself up as a candidate.

Which was his right, of course. But for some reason, his manner made her angry. Very angry. It was obvious his attitude toward her had turned around the minute he'd realized she had children. So he hated kids. No problem. She would keep her kids away from him as much as humanly possible. It was really none of her business, after all.

But only a true jerk of a man would be able to dislike her boys! It made her furious.

She thought of her own father for a moment. He had always been wonderful to her, the perfect dad. Her parents had moved to Texas years ago and she saw them much too rarely now. Adopted as a baby by the older couple, she'd probably been showered with twice the love the average child had. She just couldn't understand a man like Michael not responding to children. Good thing she'd resolved after that first night to give him as wide a berth as possible.

The good thing was, with her avoiding him and him avoiding her, they didn't have to deal much with each other. She could go to work with the confidence that she wasn't going to have to be nice to him if she didn't want to. And that was something, after all.

* * *

Only an hour and a half later, she was eating her words. And acting very nice indeed. She looked across the wide polished desk to where Michael Greco was sitting back and gazing at her like the lord of the manor, and she gave him her very best smile.

"I'm sure you understand that the last thing in the world I want is to have to ask you for a favor," she said brightly. "But the fact is, I do have to."

He was looking very bored with it all and she wanted to tell him exactly what she thought. But Leonard Trask had warned her to be nice to him. "He can break up this department if he wants to," he'd told her that very morning when she'd accidentally said something scathing about the man. "You just be careful how you act around him. He's got the ear of the big guys. We want him on our side."

"What do you need?" Michael was asking her now.

"A ride." She smiled again, though she knew her eyes weren't joining in. "My car isn't acting very reliable today. I had to take it in for repairs."

He nodded, gazing at her with what she interpreted as a speculative gleam. "Where to?"

The smile was evaporating and she was going to let it go. She just couldn't pretend. "I've been told you are going up to the site today," she said quickly. "And I need to do some research at Trivolo City Hall. So if you could just drop me—"

"You could rent a car." He was leaning back in his chair and looking as though he was enjoying this.

She clenched her fists at her sides and wondered if he noticed. "Funny you should say that," she told him, head high. "I said exactly the same thing. I sure didn't want to...bother you with this. Only Mr. Jackson in Finance shot that down in a hurry and told me to come ask you for a ride."

His eyes were sparkling with something that just might have been humor, but she couldn't be sure. Maybe it was malice, instead.

"He didn't want to pay for it, huh?" he said, leaning forward and flattening his hands on the desk surface.

"He called it a reckless disregard for prioritized resources, or something like that."

He nodded. "And he's right, of course." He glanced at his watch. "What the hell. Why don't we go ahead and leave right now?"

She hesitated. "Well, sure. Why not?"

Their gazes met for a long moment, communicating exactly why this was a very bad idea. But there was really nothing either one of them could do about it at this point. They were going to be spending some extended time together. There was no use trying to resist.

# Chapter Four

Michael's car had the sort of leather seats that seemed to reach out and pull you down inside them, holding you safe from the outside world. Char sat back with a sigh, resolved to relax if she could manage it. Leaning back, she stretched out her legs and slipped her shoes off and kneaded her toes into the thick carpeting. It was nice to be in a car that didn't jar your bones at every bump in the road, like her old rattletrap. Smooth and luxurious. She turned her head and watched the scenery fly by, determined to enjoy the ride, despite the company.

Enjoyment didn't seem like an option to Michael. He quickly realized the trip was going to be pure torture for him—the exquisite torment of trying to ignore the provocative allure of his traveling companion. And she wasn't making it any easier when she worked her crimson-tipped toes like that, letting her short skirt ride up even higher, showing off legs that were destined to star in his most erotic dreams from now on. He found himself driving too fast and breathing quickly, too. He had to put a stop to this.

"What kind of music do you like?" he asked abruptly.

She glanced at him, her startlingly blue gaze barely brushing his before looking away again. "Oh, I don't know. Anything will do. It's your car. You choose."

He chose, all right. He chose the wildest, most offensive rock and roll station he could find and put it on loud, hoping the beat could serve as a sort of wall of noise between them. It wasn't long before he knew he'd made exactly the wrong choice. He usually liked rock and he liked it loud, but he rarely listened to the lyrics. Suddenly, every lewd innuendo seemed to come through loud and clear, every suggestive come-on, every sexist metaphor. It was downright embarrassing. Even rock and roll had gone downhill. Reaching out, he quickly switched the station to a classical outlet.

"Thanks," she said, giving him a sideways grin without making eye contact. "I really like rock but that was beginning to feel like a long day in the dentist's chair."

He looked in her direction and couldn't help but smile back at her. She was right. "I just hope *this* stuff doesn't put us to sleep," he added.

"Not Vivaldi," she said serenely. "He's too gorgeous for that."

She was right again. He'd never realized how sensual classical music was before. There was something about the way she melted into the seat beside him, the way she moved and the scent from her hair, that seemed choreographed to the music. He felt like a man intoxicated by desire, but it was now a slow, subtle sort of longing that felt like pleasure instead of urgency. This he could handle. For a time, at any rate.

The Vivaldi turned to Mozart, and then to a little Ravel as they came within cruising distance of the little town of Trivolo, and the location of the White Stones project.

"Have you been up here to see the site before?" he asked her as they neared the target zone.

"No." She looked out at the blue-gray ocean sparkling in the sun to their left. "But I know this area well. I love it here."

"A lot of people love it. That's why we're developing it. So more people can come and enjoy it."

She glanced at him. "Who did they buy the land from?" she asked.

"Most of the land was being offered by Bear Creek Timber. They've had it for years." He pulled onto a dirt road. "You shouldn't have any trouble with titles on that. The ownership should be clear, though you'll need to document it. But in order to make it all work, we're going to need to convince a few small landowners along the coast to sell. Those are the titles you may have trouble validating.''

She nodded. She knew all that. She was prepared for her job. But she was luxuriating in the atmosphere. As a child, she'd roamed these beaches at will, never wondering who owned anything. Sometimes it didn't seem to pay to grow up. She smiled, thinking of her boys. She would have to bring them up here. They were old enough now that they would love playing in the waves just the way she had once.

Michael pulled the car onto the construction area on the cliff overlooking the ocean and they both got out to take a look. The ocean breeze tugged at Char's hair and she gave up, pulling out the pins to let it fly. Turning, she caught a dark look in Michael's eyes, and she realized, with a jolt, that he found her desirable. She turned away and stared out to sea, feeling uncharacteristically tongue-tied. She didn't want him to want her. But she couldn't help but feel a surge of pleasure over it. Shivering, she turned back to the car.

He followed her without a word and they drove on into town, where he dropped her in front of the small, Spanish-style city hall building.

''I'll pick you up in two hours,'' he told her gruffly, avoiding her gaze. ''That long enough for you?''

''That'll be perfect,'' she said cheerfully. ''See you then.''

She watched as he drove off, biting her lip. She'd never known a man like this before. The attraction between them almost throbbed, like...like jungle drums or something equally silly. And yet they were both trying to pretend there was nothing there. How long could this go on before some sort of disaster struck?

That question still loomed in the air two hours later. She was waiting when he drove up again, and she hopped into the car, expecting him to be morose and to drive on back to Rio de Oro without another word. But to her surprise, he had sandwiches with him.

"I thought you might be hungry," he said simply. "I was picking up something for myself. So I got you roast beef on sourdough. Is that okay?"

"Perfect." Her stomach growled. She was starving. "Are we going back to the site? We could have a picnic."

He frowned. "I thought we would just eat them in the car as we drive."

She sighed dramatically. "Just like a man. Utilitarian to the end." She picked up her sandwich and sniffed the delicious aroma. "Think of the mustard stains on the seat covers. The pickles in the carpets. The mayonnaise smears on the steering wheel."

His grin was reluctant, but for real. "Okay," he said. "You win. We'll stop at the site."

It was a small victory, but she felt good about it.

They pulled back out onto the cliff and found surveyors and construction workers in hard hats busy preparing the site for excavation. They knew Michael and nodded to Char. Once they realized a picnic was in progress, one of the men brought over a blanket for them to use.

"Can't have such a pretty lady sitting in the dirt," he said, eyeing Char with a very appealing smile. Tall and blond, he wore snug jeans and a tight T-shirt that displayed a full set of impressive muscles.

"Judd Karst, meet Chareen Wolf," Michael said, though he sounded reluctant. "Judd's the planning foreman on this phase of the operation," he added.

"Nice to meet you, Judd," Char said, responding nicely to the flirty look in the handsome foreman's eyes as he shook her hand.

"The pleasure is all mine," he said. "We don't get many beautiful women around here. I hope you'll come back and visit us often."

"You can count on it," she said, laughing up into his grin. There was nothing like flattery to make a day seem that much brighter.

As Judd walked back toward the other men, she turned to look at Michael and was shocked to see a storm cloud brewing in his gaze. Quickly, she took her place on the blanket, folding her legs sideways and tugging at her skirt to keep it from showing too much nylon-covered skin. Then she concentrated on her sandwich, but at the same time, she mused on the irony of it all. Michael didn't really want her for himself, but he still felt possessive when another man showed interest. Human nature, she supposed. But it still was odd.

She snuck a glance at him. He still looked pretty grumpy. That made her smile.

"How's your sandwich?" she asked him, licking mayonnaise off her index finger.

"Fine," he said shortly, not looking her way.

The silence stretched between them again. The sound of the waves crunching and splashing up against the sandy shore, the cry of the gulls as they fought over bits and pieces of plunder, even the light traffic on the distant highway provided a sound track to their lunch. But she wanted more.

"We could talk," she suggested, wiping her mouth with a napkin. "Get to know each other."

He frowned at her. "Why do we need to know each other?"

She suppressed a grin and waved a hand in the air. "No need, I suppose. Just a simple chat. I just thought it might be fun."

His frown darkened. "This isn't supposed to be fun. We're at work."

This time she couldn't hold the laughter back. And she made a face at him for good measure. "Oh, so that's the philosophy. No laughing during the work time. Is that it?"

His face softened. Staring at her for a long moment, he shook his head and looked back out toward the ocean. "Okay," he said gruffly. "What do you want to chat about?"

Wow, another little victory, even if he did say the word *chat* the way her little boys said *bath*. She was feeling smug, but she knew she couldn't let him know it. That would surely be the quickest way to have him heading for the car.

"Okay," she said slowly, after she'd thought it over for a moment or two. "How about this? Why do you hate kids?"

He stared at her. "You consider that light conversation?"

She put her head to the side, considering. "Not really. But it is something I want to know."

He looked away. "I don't hate kids."

She smiled and chewed thoughtfully on her last bite of roast beef and sourdough. "You give a darn good impression of a man who dislikes children," she noted calmly at last. "I've known men who liked kids a lot. They don't act like you do."

He was annoyed. She could see it in the set of his shoulders. Then he turned and said, "Look, I know you're divorced, but..."

"I'm not divorced. I've never been married."

He stopped and gazed at her quizzically. "Where's the father of those kids?"

She tucked her sandwich remains into the paper bag they came in. "I tell them he's in heaven. But I must admit, I have my doubts."

"Oh. Oh, I'm sorry."

"So am I." She smiled at him. "Mostly for their sakes. Little boys need their dads."

He nodded as though he saw her point. "You really ought to start shopping around for one, then. Don't you think?" He shrugged and looked pleased with himself. "See? I'm thinking of their best interests. I don't hate them."

"Uh-huh." She gazed at him, her eyes narrowed doubtfully. "Okay. I'll buy it. You don't hate kids. So why do you hate *women* with kids?"

He turned back and almost smiled, then looked harried. "I don't hate you, Char. In fact..."

He let the statement dangle, but his gaze was on her mouth and she felt her pulse begin to quicken.

"In fact, what?" she asked softly, knowing she was egging on something she might not be able to control.

He seemed to wince. Reaching out, he touched her cheek, just a glancing brush of his fingers against her skin, sending a shower of sensation through her. And then he was crumpling the paper that had held his sandwich and vaulting to his feet.

"We'd better get going," he said briskly.

She sat where she was, resisting the impulse to press the palm of her hand to where his fingers had touched. Slowly, she began cleaning up her own remnants. She knew he was waiting to pull up the blanket, but she needed a moment before she faced him again. Why did she have such a strong reaction to everything he did? It wasn't like her to be thrown for a loop by any man, and she didn't like it at all. As she rose, she looked out at the sea, in order to avoid looking into his eyes. And she saw something wonderful.

"Look!" she said, pointing. "Whales."

He turned as though he thought she was pulling his leg, but his face soon changed as he looked out at the huge animals swimming offshore. "Wow. Those *are* whales."

"Sure." She shaded her eyes and squinted at them. "I don't know what kind. It's a little late for blue whales. They usually forage around here in the summer."

He was still awestruck. "What fantastic creatures."

"Aren't they? I'll bet those are gray whales already on their way down to Mexico for the winter. They'll be coming back up this way in the spring."

"That is spectacular," he said, shaking his head. "Makes you feel a part of nature or something."

A part of nature. She shivered again. Maybe that was just exactly the problem.

Once back in the car, he didn't turn toward the highway as she expected.

"I want to take a run down past the houses along the beach," he told her. "That's our problem zone—the area with the holdouts."

She watched as they cruised into a familiar neighborhood. "Ohmigosh," she cried, delighted. "I didn't realize it was so close to where my uncle lives. I used to rule these beaches when I was young.''

The long row of little windswept houses stretched from one end of the shore to the other, the last line before the ocean. Each was surrounded by mounds of ice plant but not much else in the way of flora. Most plants didn't do very well in this salty environment. Built in the twenties or thirties as vacation hideaways, the cabins hardly looked ready to withstand a good stiff breeze, let alone the sort of storms that could sweep off the ocean at times. And yet they had stood for three-quarters of a century. Now, however, they were about to go.

It was a little sad. She tried to think of the new structures that would take their place. She knew what TriTerraCorp could do and she knew it would be wonderful—very upscale and trendy. Everyone would be crazy about it. Still, something would be lost.

Most of the houses already had the melancholy empty air of structures abandoned by their owners and about to be demolished. Turning, she tried to see her uncle's but it was in the opposite direction from where they were driving.

''They're really just dumps,'' Michael said, stopping between two of them in a parking place that had probably served thousands of beach-goers over the years, though there was no one in sight today. ''They're eyesores, really.''

Suddenly Char's vision was swimming in tears.

"They're beautiful eyesores," she said, jerking open the car door and stepping out onto the sand. A hundred memories flooded her, memories of sunny summer days and sunburns and campfires and Fourth of July sparklers. She could almost smell the suntan lotion. "I miss them already."

Frowning, Michael turned off the engine and followed her as she walked slowly down toward the shoreline. He didn't understand why women's emotions seemed to bounce around like Ping-Pong balls at times. What was she so upset about? If he knew, he could do something to help her, maybe. Or talk to her at least. But she didn't give him any clues to go by. So he was at a loss.

The waves were low and rolling, sending one gentle wash of water up onto the sand after another. As he followed her down toward the water, suddenly she paused, then whirled and gave him a sassy smile, ordering "Look the other way" as she kicked off her shoes.

He wanted to grab her right then, she looked so endearing. "Why?" he asked, balling his hands into fists to keep from doing it.

She flashed him another smile. "Because I'm going to strip naked and run down the beach."

His eyebrow rose. "And you expect me to avoid watching?"

She tilted her chin at him. "I had you going for a minute there, didn't I?" she teased. "You can relax. I'm just going to take off my nylons. I want to get my feet wet.''

He looked the other way obligingly, but he was so aware of her and what she was doing, he could hardly stand it. He turned back in time to see her running for the water and he followed right behind her.

''Oh!'' she gasped as the cold ocean welcomed her in up to her knees. ''Oh, that feels so good!'' She danced in the water, kicking up spray and chasing the tide as it came in and drew back out again, laughing like a girl, playing like a teenager.

He watched her for a few moments, then took off his own shoes and socks and walked down onto the wet area just beyond the reach of the lap of the waves.

She laughed at him. ''Come on in,'' she taunted. ''I dare you!''

''I can't get bare to the knees as easily as you can,'' he said, eyeing her appreciatively.

''Sure you can.'' She kicked a splash of water his way. ''Just roll up your pant legs.''

He gave her a baleful look and she laughed. ''Come on. I dare you. In fact, I double-dare you.''

''Hey.'' He pretended to get serious. ''Hold it. Watch that double-dare stuff.''

''Why?''

''Double dares are pretty dangerous.'' He gave her a look that should have made her cower but only succeeded in making her laugh. ''If you're going to go around double-daring people, you're going to have to be prepared to take the consequences.''

"I double-double-dare you!" she cried, her hair flowing in the wind.

"That does it," he said, and without the slightest hesitation, he came charging into the water toward her, not bothering to roll up anything.

Something in the look in his eyes told her he wasn't just fooling. Shrieking, she turned to run, but it was slow-going slogging in the water and he caught her before she'd taken three steps, grabbing her and deftly flinging her up so that he held her above the water.

"Double-dare *me,* will you?" he teased, holding her steady just inches from a dousing.

"Oh, Michael, no!" she cried, but she was laughing so hard she was afraid she would get hiccups. One slip and she would be totally immersed in the cold Pacific Ocean. Just one little slip…

But he wasn't going to let that happen, and though she screamed and was very scared, deep down she knew it. When he pulled her back in against his chest and carried her back onto the dry shore, she clung to him, and the laughter died in her throat. He felt so strong. She was breathless, and not from fear.

She wanted him to kiss her. She wanted it with an urgent need that trembled inside her. As he lowered her to the sand, letting her feet get balanced, she left her arms around his neck and looked up into his hazel eyes. She heard his breath catch, felt his heartbeat speed up. She lifted her lips and he lowered his. His just barely touched hers, and then he jerked back, pulling away from her arms.

"Hey," he said lightly. "None of that."

She sighed and shook her head. "No kissing in the work time, either, huh?"

But despite her easy tone, she was chagrined. She didn't think she'd ever before had a man reject a kiss she'd been so clearly offering.

They sat in the sun-warmed sand to let their legs dry, and the tension faded quickly as they talked, and then laughed when they looked into each other's eyes.

"I can't believe you did that," Char said ruefully, looking at the mess he'd made of his clothes. "I'll bet you ruined those slacks."

"No problem." He sighed melodramatically. "I can throw them out, right along with the suit coat your kid ruined with his lollipop this morning."

She made a face. "I'm really sorry about that."

He looked at her and thought, Hey, it's worth it if I get to carry you around in return, but he didn't say it aloud. What would be the point? He had to do something, say something, that would end this constant sensual pull between them. What they had been doing wasn't working. He could only think of one thing to try.

"Okay," he said, steeling himself and looking out

at the ocean. "I'm going to be totally honest with you."

She sighed, leaning back in the sand and closing her eyes. "Do you have to?"

"Yes, I think it would be for the best." He risked one look at her, then looked quickly away. She looked good enough to ravish, and that would ruin everything.

"Oh, Lord," she said, "is this one of those 'I'm doing this for your own good' sort of things?"

"Sort of."

She sighed again. "Okay. Fire away."

He started stiffly. "I don't think it's any secret that...that..." Turning toward her, he groaned, avoiding her gaze. Reaching out, he took a strand of her silvery hair between his fingers. "Look, I want you so bad my guts are in knots," he said gruffly. "My muscles are sore from holding back, my head is aching. I go nuts every time you come near me."

She turned to look at him, staring, astounded. "Oh," she said weakly. She could tell he wasn't saying this because he liked the idea. In fact, he looked like a man in some kind of psychic pain. But if he really felt that way...

He dropped her hair and frowned, looking out at the waves. "But you see, I have to stay away from you because you are exactly the kind of woman I don't want to get involved with."

She looked away. She'd known this wasn't going

to be fun. But she hadn't realized it would be this uncomfortable. "I am?"

"You are." He sighed heavily. "You're the kind of woman who is immersed in family and raising kids. That's not my scene. It will never be. I don't want to get pulled into it in any way."

Had she asked for this? She wasn't sure. Maybe she had made it clear she wouldn't have minded a kiss or two. But she hadn't exactly offered herself up to this man for the taking. It seemed to her he was assuming a bit too much here. After all, she didn't want to get involved any more than he did.

She shrugged, letting sand run through her fingers. It was probably for the best, anyway. "Okay," she said softly.

"'Okay'?" He sounded angry. "What do you mean, 'Okay'?"

She looked at him sadly, her silky blond hair framing her face. "I promise. I won't tempt you to become a family man."

His frown darkened. "You don't understand. You have no control over the temptation part. It just is."

She frowned back, pointedly mocking him. "Then I can't do much about it, can I?"

He didn't answer, and she sighed. "Tell me this. If I were childless and living in an apartment somewhere…"

"No." He shook his head emphatically. "It wouldn't make any difference. You're no playgirl." His dark gaze caressed her, following the curve of her cheek, the line of her throat, the swelling of her lovely breasts, and he groaned silently, deep inside. He wanted her so badly, he could hardly think straight.

"You put on a good front, Char. You're cool as a cucumber on the surface." His wide mouth twisted into a bittersweet smile. "But you've got the soul of a sweet, old-fashioned girl."

"Me?" But she had a lump in her throat. How did he know these things?

"Yes, you. Beneath that wise-cracking exterior, you're so obviously made for home and hearth and making people happy...."

"So why is that a bad thing?" she asked, palms open in appeal.

"It's not a bad thing." He took one of her hands in his and his tone softened. "It's not a bad thing at all. But it's not *my* thing. And I don't want any part of it."

She stared down at their joined hands. "How do you know?"

"I've been married. I know."

He'd been married. That was news. But it made sense. He wasn't a kid, after all. Looking up, she met his gaze and asked, steeling herself against the answer, "Did you have any children?"

Something flickered in the depths of his eyes. "No," he said, but it wasn't an easy no, a simple no. His "no" had a thread of pain in it that startled her. She wanted to ask more, but his face had frozen into a mask and he pulled his hand away from hers and started to rise from the sand. Slowly, she followed him to her feet, and then back to the car. But that flickering she'd seen in his eyes, and the tone of his voice, haunted her.

There was something in his past that ate away at him and made him resist falling, even temporarily, for a "sweet, old-fashioned girl." Was she ever going to know what it was? Maybe not. Probably not. And if she knew, who could say if there would be anything she could do about it? People were pretty much formed by the time they were his age. What made her think she could wave a magic wand and transform him at this point?

And who said she even wanted to?

# Chapter Five

Michael had to stop by the legal offices some distance out of town to run some issues by the project attorney. Char went in with him, but in the end, she spent most of the time sitting back and waiting while they went over questions that had nothing to do with her work. She was leafing through a magazine, but that was just a front. Sitting there, she had plenty of time to mull over some of the things Michael had said to her on the beach.

She was revising her original opinion. She liked the man. She liked him better than any man she'd known for a long, long time. And that wasn't just because he was the most attractive specimen she'd been this close to in just about forever. There was more to it than that, and she was only beginning to sort out her feelings in order to deal with it.

To begin with, he was so darn honest. When he had turned to her and admitted the way she made him feel, she'd been stunned. Where was the casual disinterest most men affected? Where was the bravado, the facade of machismo? He'd been so open about it, she'd been stumped for anything to say herself.

And at the same time, he had deeper issues that he wasn't revealing at all. She knew she'd seen evidence of that in the troubled look in his eyes. There was something in his background behind his rather rigid views of women—something he didn't want to talk about. And that made him all the more intriguing.

But mostly she'd been impressed by the way he'd zeroed right in on the truth about her. Most people were fooled by the brash and sassy persona she put on. Men seldom looked further than the projected exterior. But Michael had seen it. He'd looked underneath and uncovered the truth about her. He might even understand her and the things that made her tick a little bit. Could that be true?

*Now, wait a minute,* she told herself skeptically. *You're taking this a little too far.*

Still, the things he'd said—the way he'd known what she really was… Heck, she usually put up such a good front that she fooled herself half the time. To have him see right through that was unusual, she had to admit.

"Lucky guess," she muttered to herself.

But she didn't really believe that. She knew it was more.

Finishing his conference with the attorney, Michael rose and turned, his hazel gaze meeting hers. A little tingling current of joy shimmered through her.

Oh, no you don't, she thought to herself sternly as she rose, as well, and preceded him to the exit. Keep your irrational exuberance to yourself.

They were soon back on the highway, but they ran into very bad traffic because of an accident, and when Char used her cell phone to call the repair shop, they said her car wasn't ready. So it was getting very late by the time they got back to Rio de Oro, and Char was getting antsy about her kids.

"They're going to be wondering where I am," she said, fidgeting. "Could you do me a big favor? Could you please...I mean, would you mind...well, would you take me to pick them up?"

He shrugged. "Sure."

She bit back laughter. Here she'd been so hesitant to ask him, and he'd answered as though it were nothing at all. Maybe she was taking this antipathy he seemed to have to her children too seriously.

Or maybe not. When he pulled his car into a parking space in front of the preschool and turned off the engine, she smiled at him.

"You want to come in with me?"

"No, thanks." He gave her a dubious look. "I'll wait out here while you wander through the many levels of Dante's inferno in there.'' He pretended to consult his watch. ''If I don't hear from you by 1800 hours, I'll send in a SWAT team.''

''Very funny.'' She gripped the door handle but she didn't open the door. ''You know what I think?'' she said, turning to look back at him. ''I think you're scared of kids.''

''What?'' He met her charge with disdain.

''That's it. You're scared.'' She could see by his reaction that she'd at least got his attention, and maybe even his consideration. ''You wouldn't dare go in where all those little crumb crunchers are swarming. Would you?''

''Don't be ridiculous.'' He waved away her charges. ''I can handle kids.''

''Can you?'' Her tone was lightly taunting and she knew it was having an effect. ''Then come with me. What do you think they're going to do, nibble away at your ankles?''

He frowned at her quite fiercely, but she was now sure that his bark was worse than his bite.

''Come on, scaredy-cat. I dare you.'' She smiled wickedly. ''I double-dare you.''

He looked at her for a long moment, then shook his head and groaned, slumping down in his seat. ''Ah, no, Char. Not the old double dare.''

''Worse. I double-*dog*-dare you.''

That last one got him. He met her sparkling gaze and he couldn't resist. For some reason, he could not stop himself. He had to stay within the range of her marvelous voice, and when she got out of the car, brimming with the confidence that he would be coming, too, he found himself getting out with her.

It was a risky move. The sound of children permeated the atmosphere, and once he was inside the gate, kids were everywhere. He gazed around, feeling a sense of distaste. Grubby, smelly, noisy little monsters, weren't they?

"Come on," Char was saying, beckoning to him from a brightly lit doorway.

He followed her into the classroom, steeling himself and wondering why he'd let himself get roped into this. Then he saw Ronnie, his red hair wild, his blue eyes huge, his mouth open in a round circle of wonder.

"Ricky, look!" Ronnie cried, pointing. "The man's here."

Char reached out to comb his hair down with her fingers. "Ronnie, sweetie, please call the man Mr. Greco. That's his name."

"Gecko!" Ronnie gave him a little salute, hand out, and a wide grin to go with it. "Hi, Mr. Gecko."

"Hi, Ronnie," he said, and he had to admit the excited greeting warmed him. Just a little. He looked at Ricky, but the boy was looking down at his wooden puzzle on the table, carefully pretending Michael didn't exist.

Suddenly he had a strange feeling he was seeing himself as a kid. In a flashback of time, he remembered feelings long suppressed. And he knew without a doubt that Ricky's studied disinterest was a cover for something hurting deep down inside.

But there wasn't time to analyze that. The teacher was a young blonde who took one look at Michael and practically swooned into his arms. She began chattering to hold his attention and didn't let up for the next five minutes. Other parents stood waiting and she concentrated all her attention on a man who hated kids.

"Go figure," Char whispered to herself, shaking her head. But she soon drew Michael over to look at the children's paintings of the day.

"These are the pictures they've made of what they want to be for Halloween," the pert little teacher told them, coming along and seemingly unable to take her eyes off Michael.

"Here's Ricky's," she said, pointing to a typical Ricky picture of himself in a tiger suit.

Char nodded appreciatively. She'd been working on those darn tiger suits for weeks. The boys had been planning for their trick-or-treat night for just as long.

"We *gotta* be tigers, Mama," Ronnie had told her from the first. "Roar!"

"And here's Ronnie's painting," the teacher chirped.

Char stared, stunned. What? There wasn't a tiger in sight on this one. Instead, there was a little stick figure boy dressed in a white shirt and dark slacks, carrying what looked suspiciously like a little brief-case in his hand.

"What is this, Ronnie?" Char asked him.

"My Hall'ween," he said happily.

"I thought you wanted to be a tiger like Ricky."

"Uh-uh." He shook his head and pointed at his painting. "I want this."

Char saw weeks of sewing going down the drain. "And just who are you supposed to be?" she asked him.

Ronnie looked at her, eyes shining. "Mr. Gecko," he said brightly, as though that were the most natural thing in the world. He grinned at Michael. "See? Like him."

Michael met her gaze over the heads of the two boys and gave her a feeble grin. "Can I help it if kids regard me as a role model?" he asked her, but his eyes told her he understood. This was not nec-essarily a good thing.

And as they wandered back out toward the car, he noticed something strange. Although the shouting and running in the halls still seemed very annoying, the two little boys he was ushering out were a couple of pretty good kids. Definitely superior to all the others. You might almost say, he sort of liked them.

Michael worked very late that night, mostly doing things that weren't really critical, just to avoid going back to the beautiful old Victorian house where he knew Char was dealing with her boys and getting ready for bed herself. He couldn't face her again so soon. To face her would mean he would have to think through what the hell he was doing. And he wasn't ready to do that. He didn't want to think over what a day they'd had together—how it had been the best day he'd had in years. He didn't want to remember how Char had looked dancing in the water, how she'd felt to his touch, how she'd tasted. He'd been happy with her in a way he hadn't thought he could be anymore. It was too dangerous to think about. He had to make himself stay away from her.

"What goes up, must come down," he reminded himself. It didn't pay to let yourself get too happy.

Finally, it was after midnight. He thought it ought to be safe by now. Walking into the house, he soaked up the quiet. The only lights still on were low and left on to keep people from breaking their necks on the stairs. Everyone was asleep. It was almost as though he was alone in the place.

A nice hot shower would burn the kinks out and wash away some of the tiredness that dogged him. Stopping in at his room, he picked up a towel and his robe and headed for the bathroom at the end of the hall. And that was when he made his first mistake. He forgot about the "knock three times and pause" rule. In fact, he didn't knock at all. Instead, he jerked open the bathroom door.

"Hey!" Char cried, hugging a big white towel to

her steaming naked body and gazing at him through the mist that filled the room. "Close the door!"

And he did. The only trouble was, he took a step before doing so and landed inside the bathroom rather than out. She stared at him and he stared at her. Her hair was wet, sticking to her rosy skin in strands. The big fluffy towel covered all the relevant areas, but the fact that she was naked beneath it was intoxicating to his senses. He'd vowed to stay away from her, but somehow fate had managed to throw her into his lap, anyway. What was a man to do? Resistance seemed futile. Dropping his own towel and robe on the counter that ran along one side of the room, he took another step toward her and reached out to catch a stream of warm water that was running down her arm with his index finger.

She looked up into his eyes and didn't back off. "I think you made a wrong turn somewhere," she noted dryly.

He grinned, cupping the back of her head in his hand as he lowered his lips to hers. "How can it be wrong when it feels so right?" he murmured, and then his mouth covered hers.

She opened to him. There was nothing shy or hesitant about her response. Her hands were busy holding the towel tightly to her body, but her mouth was his for the moment, warm and pliant and arousing. He had never tasted anything so sweet and ripe and luscious. He could have gone on kissing her for as long as he could have held off the need to take things further, but she was already pulling away.

"Country-and-western songs aside, this is not a good idea," she said a bit breathlessly.

His shirt was damp and sticking to his chest in places and he enjoyed the evidence of where he'd been. "Believe it or not, I didn't do this on purpose."

Her mouth quirked and she tossed her head. "Well, that makes all the difference, of course."

He grinned, trailing a finger down her cheek and reveling in the warmth of her skin, the heat radiating from her slinky body. "It does, doesn't it?"

"No," she answered promptly, blue eyes flashing. "It doesn't give either one of us an excuse."

One dark eyebrow rose in question. "Either one of us?" he repeated.

"Either one of us," she said simply. "Perhaps you haven't noticed, but the temptation thing is mutual. I seem to have this insane level of attraction to you."

He'd known that, but just to have her say it caused a hot feeling of deep satisfaction to spread through his chest.

"What are you talking about?" he teased. "I remember what you said about me when you didn't know I was listening. I thought you said I had a ruthless mouth."

She laughed softly. "Oh, you do."

"And my eyes are too close together."

She gave an embarrassed smirk. "Well, that was a slight exaggeration."

"What about the shifty-look thing?"

"'Shifty'?" She tried wide-eyed innocence. "I thought I said 'nifty.'"

"Right."

He was kissing her again. He couldn't stay away when she was so close. She was kissing him back and he was actually beginning to think thoughts of taking this further. He had an insatiable hunger to see every curve and cranny of her beautiful body, to run his hand over every inch, and maybe his tongue as well. He could already feel what it would be like to make love with her, to join her body with his and dig deep for that illusive fulfillment that made life worth living. He was so close. After all, it wouldn't take much to get her to drop the towel and...

"Hello? Chareen? Are you in there?"

The male voice, so close, made them both jump and jerk apart.

"Y-yes," Char answered quickly, eyes wide now with shock.

"Hi. It's Bob. Just wanted to make sure you were okay. I thought I heard voices."

Her horrified gaze met his and Michael groaned softly. It was Bob Jenks, the engineer from Santa Barbara who sometimes stayed on the second floor when he had a late assignment.

Char gathered her wits together and managed a semicoherent answer. "Oh...I was just...singing."

To Michael, she whispered, "It's like Grand Central Station around here. Do any of you realize it is after midnight?"

"That was it," she called out again. "I was singing."

"Okay," Bob called back. "You going to be much longer?"

She glanced at Michael and made a face. "Uh...no. Are you waiting for the shower?"

"No, not really. It's just—well, the water running in the pipes and all. It goes right past my bed and it sounds like a river. I heard it and I just wanted to make sure."

"Oh, I'm sorry." She gave Michael a desperate look and whispered, "What if he waits for me out there?"

Michael grinned and whispered back. "Then we'll just walk out together like two grown-ups."

"In your dreams!" she hissed at him. Aloud, she called out, "Well, everything's okay."

"Okay," he answered. "Well, good night."

"Good night," she called hopefully.

Footsteps sounded, loud at first, then fading along the floorboards. She looked at Michael, her eyes shooting daggers. "Now see what you've done?" she whispered.

Michael was trying hard not to laugh aloud. "I haven't done anything. It's old insomniac Bob out there, skulking around in the halls, looking for women...."

"This is not funny," she said, eyes darkening as she began to realize how this meeting might look to others. "After all, I've got my kids to think about. I can't be having sexy encounters with my kids just a few feet away. It isn't right." She looked at him for understanding of her position.

But Michael felt stung by her tone and he answered defensively. "I didn't realize you were such a moralist," he muttered.

"Just one of my odd little idiosyncrasies," she snapped, glaring at him. "We sweet, old-fashioned girls are like that."

"You're making my point for me, aren't you?" he said coolly.

She turned away, disappointed. Was he really just like any other man, only on the lookout for a quick roll in the hay? She'd thought he was different. Reaching for her robe, she turned her back to slip into it, pulling the sash into a tight knot at the waist.

"I'm getting out of here. Stand back so no one can see you when I open the door."

"Whatever you say."

He watched her go, watched the door close with a finality that seemed symbolic, and he said a hard oath under his breath. But, what the hell? He deserved it. He'd known better than to mess with a woman like Char. He'd known from the beginning exactly where her loyalties lay. What had he expected to happen, after all?

This only confirmed his conviction that he should stay away from her. Far, far away.

But there was the morning breakfast promise to get through. True to her word, Hannah had cooked her heart out and Michael couldn't insult her by hurrying through the meal. Instead, he enjoyed it.

The room was bright with sunlight streaming in through the lacy curtains. Green place mats, beautiful yellow china, heavy sterling silver flatware, a vase full of orange Iceland poppies in the center of the table, all combined to give the morning a special feel.

"Hannah, you've got a mind like a steel trap," he told the older woman, making her beam with pleasure. "You've fixed me every one of the items that I mentioned to you yesterday. Didn't leave a thing out."

She popped another helping of French toast on his plate. "When it comes to fixing food for people, I know my business."

"You certainly do. This is delicious."

He'd come down early, hoping to get this over with and be out the door before the rest of the house arrived for breakfast. But the food was so good, he was still hanging around, even as the others began to drift into the room. There was nothing like a satisfying meal to bring on a feeling of well-being— even when it wasn't deserved.

He was just about to reluctantly get up and leave,

when Char ushered her boys into the room, and he realized he'd better stay for a few more minutes, or his departure would look a little strange. Char gave him a fleeting smile just before she sat in her chair, but after that her attention was all on her children.

He knew he should go, but he was feeling so mellow after his wonderful breakfast that he lingered over coffee and found himself chatting with two other boarders at the table, one an engineer from Dallas named Ralph Boortz, and the other a contract worker from Seattle named Simon Jeter. But his attention was on Char and the way she was dealing with the boys. She was a damn good mother from what he could see of it. Just why that made him feel proud of her, he wasn't sure. After all, that was part of what had warned him off the night before.

"Those two redheads remind me of my boys at home," Ralph said as he grinned at Ricky's attempt to balance a spoon on his nose. "Boy, I sure do miss them. Hope to get home to see them in about a week or so."

"How many do you have?" Char asked him as she deftly took the spoon and put it out of Ricky's reach.

"I've got two boys, too. *And* three girls."

"Oh, my, a whole crew."

"Yeah. We have a great time. They're all good kids. Everywhere we go we're like a small herd moving through."

Char smiled at him. "I've always wanted a whole passel of kids, too. Six was once my goal." She chuckled, remembering. "I'd especially like to have a girl or two myself. But I'm pretty happy with these two."

"How about you, Greco?" Ralph asked in a friendly manner. "Got any kids?"

"No," he said shortly, taking a long sip of coffee.

But his mind was still on Char's answer. So she wanted a passel of kids. He should have known she would. If he was still kidding himself about there being any chance at all of a relationship with her, that certainly nipped it in the bud. His mood, which had been so mellow, turned ugly, and something began tying his stomach into knots.

"Mr. Greco isn't a 'kid person,' as he is constantly informing me," Char said. Her glance touched his and then skittered away.

"Well, that's too bad," Ralph commiserated in his hearty way. "What happened? An unhappy childhood or something?" He shook his head, not seeming to expect an answer. "That'll do it," he told Char. "I once had a friend who hated kids. Turned out he'd been abused when he was young."

"I wasn't abused," Michael said icily, wiping his mouth with the napkin and rising from his chair. "Everything doesn't conform to the junk-psychology that's popular on TV talk shows," he added. "Some things just are."

He caught Char's gaze as he left the room, and for one tense moment he thought she saw right through his pretense. But then he realized she couldn't possibly. How could she know what it had been like for him as a child? He'd lied when he'd said he wasn't abused. Abuse could be emotional. It didn't have to display wounds that bled. He knew damn well his problems today stemmed from his childhood. But you couldn't change what had happened to you. So who the hell cared, anyway?

Anger burned in him, but in the next few moments, something happened that put it out like a bucket of water on a campfire flame. He rounded the corner to where he'd left his things in the foyer, and there was Ronnie, who had obviously sneaked out ahead of him, holding his briefcase with two hands wrapped around the handle.

"Here you go," Ronnie said, smiling sweetly at him. "Go to work, Mr. Gecko!"

Michael took the case from the child and looked down at him, suddenly feeling as though something were swelling in his chest. "Thanks, Ronnie," he said. His voice was just a little shaky and he had to resist an impulse to ruffle the kid's hair. "See you tonight."

"See you tonight," Ronnie echoed, and raced to the window seat where he could watch the front walk.

Michael was aware of the boy watching him all the way to the car, and just before he got in, he turned and waved. Ronnie waved back. And why that put a smile on his face and a song in his heart, he didn't know. But he was humming to himself all the way to work.

# Chapter Six

An agreement was never spoken between them, but Char knew as well as Michael did that they were going to stay away from each other from now on.

That was really a shame. As a man, he appealed to her as no other man ever had, even Danny. But she was so much older now, so much wiser, and she knew it took more than love and sex to make a relationship work. Michael had trouble deep in his soul and it got in the way. If he couldn't wrestle it into submission, she knew she would have to deal with it herself in order to get it out of the way. And since she didn't have a clue what it might be, there wasn't much hope of doing that. So there it sat and there it would stay.

"Too bad," she murmured to herself, fighting a sinking sensation in her midsection as she watched him leave the building with one of the vice presidents for lunch the next day. He was gorgeous to look at, but much too dangerous to touch.

But she had plenty of things to deal with herself and she didn't have time to moon over him. Her car was repaired, and her house should be ready to move back into soon, as well. Then she would only have to see him at work, and that wouldn't be so bad. She had to admit, it was hard lying in her cold, lonely bed at night and thinking of him only two walls away.

*Still,* she would tell herself scornfully, *what would you do with him if you had him here?* There was no point in dallying with a man who had nothing but a little extracurricular lovemaking in mind. And there was never any use thinking you were going to change a man's mind by making him fall so deeply in love with you that he would change himself for you. Did that ever happen except in love stories? *Hah!*

Better that they should keep their distance from each other. There was no doubt they were physically attracted. The electricity that zapped between them whenever they were in the same room almost made her hair stand on end. That was something they would just have to get over. She was going to remain on guard against stray emotions that could get her into trouble.

But if she didn't see much of the man himself, she certainly heard a lot about him. Rumors were flying around the third floor where she spent most of her time. Much of the gossip concerned young women who were sure a smile from Michael meant he was on the verge of asking them out—and hope was certainly running high.

But there were also whisperings about his prospects of getting the vice presidency everyone seemed to know he wanted. He had some competition, it seemed. Gillette Johnson, the financial manager, thought he was next in line and he hadn't been shy about spreading that view to others.

Four or five members of the executive board, which sat in Florida, were due in Rio de Oro to take a look at how things were going. The word was that they would be weighing Michael's performance so far in the balance and reporting back to the full board on his progress. Good old Gillette was going all out, making his people work overtime to make sure their end of the operation shone like a diamond. In contrast, they said that Michael was taking the competition rather casually. Char wasn't sure if that meant he was just supremely confident—or basically rather arrogant. There was no doubt that he wasn't working at it as hard as Gillette was. Still, the smart money seemed to be on Michael.

She tried to ignore it all and keep her mind on her job. After all, he was only her temporary boss. She had no claim to him and he obviously had no further interest in her.

She did have to meet with him occasionally. And

in one of those meetings, while going over some land titles, she heard some other news that stunned her.

She'd gone into his office reluctantly, knowing her heart would skip a beat when she saw him—and it did. He looked so handsome with his brow furled over some problem on the desk before him, his hair slightly tousled, the knot in his tie tugged to one side. He looked up and their eyes met, and for a moment, the entire room seemed to fade away. There was something in his eyes, something that seemed to see into hers in a way no other man had ever done, and for just a moment, she felt a yearning that was almost pain.

But he shut it down immediately and nodded as though she were someone he barely knew. "Sit down, Chareen," he said briskly. "We've got a problem and I want you to be aware of the ramifications."

She dropped into a chair beside his desk and noticed, with a tiny, guilty thrill, that he couldn't resist glancing at her legs as she crossed them. "What's up, boss?" she asked.

He pushed a typed list across the desk to where she could see it. "We're going to have to do something about the squatters."

She leaned forward, studying the addresses on the list. "The holdouts along that strand of beach?"

"Exactly. I've met with them three times. They're a hardheaded bunch."

"And they're still holding out?" She flashed him a sympathetic smile. "I'm surprised you haven't convinced them to give it up."

He sighed, running his fingers through his hair and grimacing. Watching him, she felt a strong urge to reach out and comb his hair down again with her fingers, just as she would for one of her boys. Her mouth quirked as she thought of what his reaction might be if she did such a thing. It was almost worth the effort to find out.

But he didn't seem to notice her interest in his hair. "I've got the town side cleaned out," he said, his face set in serious contemplation. "But it's that last little area by the pier that has me stumped. We're going to have to get tough, I'm afraid."

By the pier. A sudden tingle of premonition slid down her spine. "Really?" she said weakly, looking back at the addresses and trying to remember...

"It's only five houses, but they are crucial. I have no doubt I could convince most of them. But not the leader. He's a raging idiot and he's got the rest of them cowed."

Char swallowed hard. "What's his name?" she asked, pretty sure she knew. "It wouldn't be Zachary Palmer, by any chance?"

He frowned at her. "Yes. Do you know him?"

"He's my uncle." She laughed uncomfortably. "Oh, my gosh, I had no idea!" But of course, she should have known.

"Oh." Michael looked interested. He sat up taller

in his chair. "Well, this is a stroke of luck. You're going to have to talk to him. Make him give it up."

"Me? Talk to Uncle Zach?" She laughed and shook her head. "I don't think so."

"Why not?"

"If Uncle Zach is leading some sort of revolution… I mean, it would be right down his alley to do something like that."

She laughed again, but Michael didn't seem to think it was very funny. His brows were coming together in a threatening way and his gaze had definitely hardened.

"This is a real problem, you know," he told her.

She shrugged and gave him a sunny smile. "Twisting arms is not within my job description."

"I'm not asking you to twist arms. All I'm asking is that you talk to the man."

She knew he was getting angry with her. After all, this project was very important to him. From what she understood, his promotion was pretty much riding on how well he handled White Stones.

But that was not something she could really do anything about. Zach Palmer was a real character and he'd never listened to anyone else in his life. She could remember well the arguments her parents had gotten into with him over the years. The moment you told Zach to do one thing, you could be sure he would do just the opposite, just to be ornery. And, much as she knew he loved his niece, he wasn't about to take advice from any young greenhorn who hadn't lived half as long as he had on this earth.

That was Uncle Zach's way. Unfortunately, she didn't think she could do anything to help Michael. And she certainly couldn't make any promises. She began collecting her things together for a quick get-away.

He rose when she did, stopping her with a hand on her arm. For just a moment, her eyes met his and she felt something slip deep inside. But his fingers tightened on her arm and he said, "Will you talk to him?"

She cleared her throat and said, "No."

His hand fell away and she turned on her heel and left the office.

She'd said no, and in a way, she meant it. But she knew in her heart that she would be going up to find out what the heck was going on very soon. And what would she actually say to her uncle...who knew?

She got her chance the very next day. She came across some details that could only be verified by a trip to the city hall in Trivolo to go over some old land titles from the eighteenth century. She drove up early, getting her work in the government office done in fifteen minutes, and then headed out to the beach.

The area looked even bleaker than it had the week before. Most of the houses were not only empty, but they looked as though someone had come by and taken just about anything that wasn't nailed down.

Her uncle's house was one of the few exceptions. Curtains still fluttered in the windows and she could see furniture through the dirty glass in the door. But no one answered when she knocked.

She made her way around the little house, letting memories dance in her head as she saw things she recognized. It had been so long since she'd seen her uncle. How could she have let so much time go by? When she'd been young, she'd spent her summers here. But once she'd grown up and her parents had moved to Texas, she'd hardly seen him more than once or twice a year. She wondered if he even remembered that she worked for the company that was planning to take his house away.

"Chareen Wolf! Is that you?"

Char whirled, stared at the older woman coming down the sand toward her, then broke into a run and greeted her with a hug. "Annie May!" she cried. "How are you?"

"Just fine, darling." Annie May smiled, set down the bundles she was carrying and pushed her graying hair back out of her eyes with a work-worn hand. "I haven't seen you since your babies were just born."

Char shrugged helplessly. Annie May had known about Danny and had been sympathetic from the beginning. "I've been busy trying to keep things together. You know how that is."

"Don't I just?"

They smiled at each other, enjoying just being in sight of someone from a well-loved past.

"What are you doing?" Char asked her, looking at the bags and box she'd been carrying.

"Moving out. Getting out of the way for the big resort project they are putting in here."

Char sighed. "I work for TriTerraCorp," she said simply.

Annie May frowned. "You know, I had forgotten that." And then she laughed. "Oh, Lord, don't remind your uncle."

Char laughed with her, but ruefully. "I hear he's quite the community activist these days."

"Oh, yes he is. He's got his little gaggle of followers and they are marching around yelling 'Hell no, we won't go' just like it was the sixties all over again. Only this time, they mean they won't let TriTerraCorp have their property."

Char glanced toward Annie May's shell of a house. "But you sold to them, didn't you?"

"Sure. This old place was falling down around my ears as it was. I was happy to be bought out. I'm living with my daughter and her family up by the old golf course. They've got a real nice house. I'm doing okay."

Char shook her head. "So you're not one of Uncle Zach's army, huh?"

"Oh, no. Life is too short to spend it tangling with lawyers."

Char laughed and picked up one of Annie May's bundles, helping her carry it to her car. She was sorry she'd missed her uncle, but she would come back again soon.

After saying goodbye to her friend, she drove up and stopped at the cliff-top site, wondering if the men who'd been surveying the week before might be there. She wouldn't have minded seeing that handsome Judd again. But there was no one there, and as she stood on the windswept lot, she looked out on a dark and gloomy day of fog and mist and cold that was nothing like the sunny day of last week when she and Michael had sat on the ground and had their picnic in this same spot. For a moment, she almost had a lump in her throat. Funny to be nostalgic about something only a few days old— something that would probably never happen again.

*But there you go,* she thought to herself. *The human mind is a strange and wonderful thing.*

"Give it up," she said aloud, and kicked a rock with her soft leather shoe, immediately regretting it. The rock sailed a few feet and clattered down into the dirt. Her shoe showed a scuff that wasn't going to go away easily. "Oh, why do I do these things?" she moaned. Getting back in her car, she drove back to Rio de Oro as fast as she dared.

Luckily, she made it back in time to keep a lunch date she had with Kyra Symington Redman and Gayle Smith Marin, both good friends who had worked at TriTerraCorp back in the days when Char was making her way up the paralegal ladder. They met at the Myrtle Turtle and clinked their tall fruit drinks cheerfully as they exchanged stories of what was going on in their lives these days. Both Kyra and Gayle had recently married and had little ones to care for. Pictures were passed around and exclaimed over, and laughter served to smooth over some of the disappointments of Char's recent days. In fact, she hardly thought about Michael until Kyra brought him up.

"Hey," her friend said, raising one sleek eyebrow. "I hear your new boss is a hunk."

Char choked on her bite of seared fish and took a drink of water before asking, "What are you talking about?"

"Your Mr. Michael Greco. I hear he is really something. And I saw his picture in a calendar of TriTerraCorp hunks. Looks like rumors are true for once."

Char stared at Kyra. "You saw his picture in a calendar?"

Kyra nodded.

"No, you couldn't have. Sherry promised to take his picture out."

"I saw it just this morning when I dropped by my old office. It was definitely in."

Char let her breath out in a slow breeze, her mind working. From what she knew of Michael, and from what she'd heard about his ambitions, she had a feeling this was not going to be something he would laugh off. She had a meeting with him later in the afternoon—a meeting he'd called for without letting her know what he wanted to discuss. Should she warn him? Or did he know already?

"Oooh. I don't think he's going to like that," she murmured, leaving the rest of her lunch untouched.

The other two women went on eating and talking about their families, but Char's mind was full of worry about Michael. And at the same time, she was annoyed at herself for caring. What was he going to do about this once he found out?

She didn't have long to wait to find out if she was right. Her phone was ringing as she walked into her office about an hour later. It was Lena Harold, Michael's secretary.

"Hi, Char. I know you've got a meeting planned for later, but…can you get down here right away? The boss is in rare form. Maybe you can do something to calm the savage beast."

"What happened?"

She hesitated. "You'd better come see for yourself."

Uh-oh. What had she done now? Was this about her uncle? Or was it the calendar situation?

She hurried down to Michael's office. And sure enough, Lena was thumbing through a calendar with a look of pure amazement on her face. When Char came in, she looked up and grinned. "Take a look at this,'' she said, dangling the calendar before her eyes.

Despite knowing exactly what to expect, Char gasped. Sherry had promised to take Michael's picture out, but there it was, big as life and sexier than ever. Seeing it now, and knowing Michael better, she could see that the picture embodied a lot that was true about the man. His own build wasn't a whole lot less impressive than the phony one Sherry had attached to Michael's head. The eye patch gave him a jaunty air that fit his humorous personality, and the pirate costume added flair. All in all, it was quite an exciting picture. She could imagine just about every woman at TriTerraCorp drooling over it at this very moment.

''Copies of this calendar are flying all over the building,'' Lena told her, confirming her fears. ''Unfortunately, some of the big boys have seen it. There's going to be a meeting of the board on it tomorrow.''

''The board?'' Char cried, dismayed.

Lena nodded. ''They arrived this morning. And good old Gillette Johnson made sure they saw this, first thing. Mr. Strand is furious. Rumor is, Michael is going to be raked over the coals for participating.''

''But he didn't.'' Char shook her head, thinking back. ''It wasn't his fault.''

Lena shrugged. ''The board wants to know who

is behind it.'' She gave Char a sideways look. "You know, don't you?''

Char frowned at her, then began shaking her head. "Oh, no, I can't..." She let the sentence dangle and gazed helplessly at the older woman.

Lena's green eyes narrowed. "Be realistic, sweetie,'' she said carefully. "And think about Michael. This is someone who thinks he's going to be a vice president someday. Someone who's now been passed around in the hands of all the employees in this outlandish pirate outfit...''

"But that's not his fault!''

"And you could tell the board about that.''

Char thought for a moment, frowning, but she didn't see a way out. "I don't see how I can rat on those women,'' she said, looking up at Lena.

"Your choice.'' Lena shrugged again. "But it's been my experience that when this many of the top guys are mad, someone has to pay the piper.'' She shook her head and gave Char a wise look over her glasses. "You watch out. You don't want to be the one thrown to the wolves.''

Char winced. "Is he in?'' she asked.

Lena nodded. "He's waiting for you.''

Squaring her shoulders, Char headed for the door to Michael's office.

Michael put down the psychology text he'd been skimming and leaned back in his chair, rubbing his neck. Closing his eyes, he worked his shoulders, trying to loosen muscles gone tight with uneasiness. He kept thinking things would get easier, but they just got more and more weird.

He was waiting for Char. She ought to be here any minute. He had a few things he needed to talk to her about—mainly this calendar thing—and some more personal business. And he wasn't looking forward to it.

Char. If he'd known that first day what a problem she was going to be...he'd have done what, exactly? Insisted on a different paralegal? Probably not. But he might have avoided living in the old Victorian that threw them together day after day.

What was it about the woman that stuck to him like a burr and wouldn't let him be? There was that sultry voice, of course. And the way she walked. And her pretty face. And...

Hell, he had to stop thinking about her like this. Sometimes he felt as though he were possessed. He'd managed to gain a certain amount of distance from her during the day, but at night, she was all he thought about.

The funny thing was, while he had been doing a relatively good job of cooling things with Char, things had only warmed between him and her two kids. Even Ricky had begun to come around from time to time. He liked the little guys. What could he say? It was the first time in his life he'd gotten to know boys of that age. These two were probably a lot better than most.

He'd never thought about kids one way or another until after he'd married Grace. He'd married her knowing how much she wanted a big family, and that had been okay with him. He hadn't really even considered what that would mean.

Until he'd realized they couldn't have children of their own. Suddenly, it had become all-important. Just seeing other people with children had hurt. As Grace's unhappiness had grown, so had his bitterness and resentment. He'd convinced himself that he didn't like kids at all. But now, as he was getting more honest with himself, he realized that had never really been the problem. He'd cultivated a dislike of kids so that he wouldn't have to deal with them, because to interact with them had been to remind himself of his own sterility. And that meant failure, in Grace's eyes, and in his own.

But it was different with Char's kids. He could be around them and not be reminded of anything but the fact that kids were funny and sometimes even fun to be around.

On Sunday, he'd spent the afternoon doing some odd jobs around the old Victorian for Hannah. He'd changed a couple of light bulbs and fixed the lock on the bathroom door—now that everyone was complaining about it—and adjusted a burner on the old gas stove.

Ronnie had followed him around the entire time, holding tools and saying, "What's that?" so often, he'd have thought it would have driven him crazy. But for some reason, it didn't.

On Monday morning, when he'd stopped at the usual magazine stand to get a paper, he'd hesitated as his gaze fell on the magazines for kids, and on impulse, he asked the vendor to recommend a comic book young boys would like.

"Anything bloody and gory," the old man told him. *"Tangleweeds, Platinum Heart, The Badger..."*

"I think they're a little young for those. Anything a little less...violent?" he'd asked quickly, picturing Char's face if he showed up with comics depicting tattooed angels.

"Uh, sure. Winnie the Pooh. Just got a new series of them in."

Michael had bought two, one for each boy. But later that day, when he got them back to the house, he wondered what the hell he was doing. Would Char think he was making overtures if he gave the comic books to her kids? Maybe it would be better just to dump them in the trash. Or leave them lying around somewhere.

But he got his chance after dinner when he found the boys playing in the hallway outside his room. Char was nowhere in sight. He watched them for a moment. They were making plenty of noise, but they were as cute as puppies. Without giving himself time to think it through, he reached into his room and grabbed the comics.

"Hey, guys," he said. "Do you like comic books?"

The boys eyed them, then Ronnie took his and grinned at Michael. Ricky looked out of the corner of his eye, but then turned away as though he wasn't interested.

"Hey, thank you, mister," Ronnie said, and plopped down on the floor cross-legged to look at his. Ricky stared at the wall.

"I'll put yours here, Ricky," Michael said, and placed it on the floor of the hallway. "You can get it later."

But watching the boy broke his heart. He could see himself acting very much the same way at just a little older age than Ricky. *Don't ever let them see you cry.* That old phrase popped into his head as he went into his room and closed the door. That was what he'd learned as a kid once he'd realized that the man he'd called his father didn't give a damn about him anymore.

When he went out later, the comic was still lying on the floor, but when he came back just before midnight, it was gone. Perhaps Ricky had picked it up and read it, after all.

As he lay in bed that night, staring at the ceiling and thinking about Char, he realized something disturbing. Instead of getting rid of his obsession with the woman, he'd added her kids to his inventory. This was not a good sign. The only way out was to finish the White Stones project and get out of town.

A knock sounded on his office door, jarring him back to the present, and in another minute Char was walking in, looking wary.

"You wanted to see me?" she said, and her chin rose as though she was already defending herself against some sort of unfair accusation.

He nodded. "Sit down."

She did, but she didn't smile. There was a blush to her cheeks that made her look as though she'd just come in out of the sun. He liked the way her blond hair caught the light, how it flowed down her back, how stray strands flared around her face. But enough of that. If he let himself get bogged down in appreciation of Char, he would never get anywhere.

"You've seen the calendar?" he said, getting right to the point.

She nodded.

He raised his hand, palm up. "What happened?" he demanded. "I thought your friend was going to keep me out of it."

She opened her mouth to say something, looking very much as though she was going to snap back at him, and then she hesitated, and closed it. Taking a deep breath, she started again.

"I'm sorry. I thought the same thing you did. I guess one of us should have followed up to make sure the picture got deleted."

He noticed she was carefully spreading blame around. But he also knew that she was friends with the woman who had put together his picture in the first place.

"What's her name?" he asked shortly.

She looked at him innocently. "Who?"

"You know very well who. The woman who stole my picture from Human Resources and put it in the calendar."

She looked uncomfortable. "Why do you want her name?"

"I need her name. She's the one who's behind all this, and she's the one who can tell the board that I had nothing to do with it. She and those other two who were with her."

She wasn't meeting his gaze any longer and he was beginning to have a bad feeling about that. Not only was she acting much too nervous for comfort, she was also taking much too long to answer him.

"Michael, there's no point in bringing them into this. Just tell the board you had nothing to do with it, that it's all a joke, and leave it at that. It's just a silly calendar."

He was still giving her that level stare. "The names, Char. All I need is the names."

Her mouth was dry. She looked down at her hands, then glanced around the office nervously. This wasn't easy. But she didn't know what else she could do.

"I'm sorry, Michael," she said at last, raising her bright blue gaze to meet his. "I'm really very, very sorry. But I'm not going to be able to tell you their names."

# *Chapter Seven*

Michael sat for a moment, stunned. It hadn't occurred to him that Char might do such a thing as this. He had to know the names. Didn't she understand how important this was?

"Why not?" he asked, more in a sort of perverse curiosity than anger at this point.

"I won't be the one who turns them in," she said flatly.

"Turns them in?" He stared at her, incredulous. "They're not going to jail over this," he said.

She glanced at him, then away. "No. But they very well might lose their jobs."

He shook his head, not getting it. "Well, you know, people should be willing to stand behind what they do. And if you mess up, you should take the consequences."

"I...I agree with that in theory." She stopped, then finally looked him straight in the eye, and suddenly she was pleading with him. "But...oh, listen, Michael. Two of those women are hanging on to their jobs by their fingernails. They've skated the last two layoffs, but just barely. One of them has three children and no husband. The other has a sick mother to support. I'm not going to do anything to help jeopardize those jobs." She searched his eyes for understanding. "If it was something that I thought had really hurt anyone, I'd report them in a heartbeat. But I don't think this is a case of real harm. To anyone but...but you."

His heart felt like a stone. "And I obviously don't count with you at all."

"That's not true. You count very much." She was flushing, but he was thoroughly annoyed with her and not receptive to that message right now. She could see that, and she could hardly blame him. There was hardly any point in going on and on about it. "And I'm sorry it has come to this. But this is where I stand."

"I think you're being ridiculous."

He gazed at her coldly, and she rose to go.

"You have your opinion," she said wearily, "I have mine."

"Obviously." But his anger faded as he thought of something else. "Wait. Don't go yet. We still have that other matter to discuss."

He hesitated, wondering if this was really the

right time to bring this up. But it wasn't often that he caught her alone without her children lately. Taking a deep breath, he pushed her obstinance over the calendar out of his mind and pulled his blood pressure back down to normal. "I had a specific reason I wanted to see you this afternoon. Something other than the calendar."

She sat back down in the chair, looking skittish, tugging on the hem of her skirt to make sure it didn't ride up too far. Watching her, he had to admit, it was hard to be angry when she looked so endearing.

"What is it?" she asked, looking rather anxiously into his eyes.

He folded his hands before him on the desk. This was not an easy subject to bring up, but he felt it had to be done. "I want to talk to you about Ricky."

She looked bewildered. "Ricky? What about him?"

This was hard, much tougher than he'd thought it would be. The right words were eluding him. "Listen, I've been doing some research," he began, putting his hand on the book he'd been reading.

Char glanced at the book, reading the title, *The Withdrawn Child: Reasons and Remedies*. She frowned, more puzzled than ever.

"And as a matter of fact, I've had some experience with this sort of thing. I think you need to get help."

She stared at him, and he could see that she was beginning to understand what he was talking about.

But she wasn't reacting well. In her eyes was the growing realization that Michael thought there was something wrong with her son.

"Wait a minute," she said defensively. "Just because Ricky doesn't adore you the way Ronnie does doesn't mean there's something wrong with him."

"It's more than that, Char. I've watched him with other people at the house. It's not just the way he responds to me."

Her head went back and her eyes hardened. "I can't believe this. You waltz into our lives, take one look and start diagnosing our little peculiarities. Where do you get off?"

He took a deep breath and tried to think of how he could deflect her anger. If she just got mad, he wouldn't be able to get anywhere with this. "I know this is hard to hear, Char, but I think you've got a problem with Ricky and you need to get some help. Therapists can do…"

He didn't get any further. Char was up and out of her chair and spitting fire.

"How dare you!" she cried, outrage quivering around her like an aura. "What do you know about my son? What right do you have to say anything about him?"

He rose, too. "Char, wait. Let me tell you why—"

"You can't tell me a damn thing," she said with even anger. "There is nothing wrong with my son. Don't you think I'd know if there was something wrong? I'm his mother. And I'll thank you to mind your own business.''

Michael groaned softly as she strode from the office and swore under his breath. He'd messed that up royally. Now what? All he wanted was to help Ricky. How could he convince Char of that?

He'd have to try to talk to her again. Somehow, he had to get through to her. He was actually surprised at how much he cared about this—but he did care. And it didn't even have anything to do with how he felt about Char. His concern was all wrapped up in the welfare of one little boy who was in pain and needed help—and another boy who had dealt with a similar pain all alone.

Char was in the kitchen early that evening, right after feeding her boys, when Michael walked in, looking for some ketchup for the cheeseburger he'd just picked up at a fast-food stand. He glanced her way, nodded and went about his business. She was waiting for water to boil for her tea and so she was stuck there, staring at his back. His attitude seemed to her a very large, silent reproach. She was sure he was wondering why she wouldn't ever do anything he wanted her to do. And truthfully, she felt guilty about it.

She'd spent most of the time since she'd left his office worrying about the things he'd said. She knew he had a point. If she were honest with herself, she would have admitted long ago that Ricky was awfully introverted for a boy his age. But to admit that was to start down the road of doing something about it. And since she had a gut feeling that it had more to do with the lack of a man in his life than anything else, what exactly was she supposed to do?

Still, Michael had been trying to help—in his own rather clumsy way. She shouldn't have reacted quite so harshly. He meant well. But that didn't mean she was ready to talk her son over with this man who knew nothing about it.

On the other hand, she felt as though she owed him more of an explanation about the calendar issue. And maybe her refusal to intercede with her uncle, as well. She took a step toward him and touched his arm.

"Michael, I wish you'd let me explain. About the calendar thing."

He glanced back, barely taking her in, then looking away again. "No need. I get it."

"You get what?"

"I understand." He put the top back on the ketchup bottle and turned toward the refrigerator to put it away. "I can see what your priorities are. And there's no reason why I should be one of them."

Her shoulders sagged and her stomach dropped. He hated her. She could tell. And maybe she deserved being hated. After all, she hadn't done much to brighten his day lately. And he was her boss.

"I hate being in this position," she told him fretfully. "I hate putting you in this position."

He turned to look her full in the face, his eyes cool and wary. "Don't worry about it. You're not the only person in that building who knows who put out the calendar. We'll get to the bottom of it without your help."

She groaned. "Tell that to the board," she said sardonically.

"What do you mean?" he said, frowning.

"They've called me in to appear tomorrow."

He gazed at her for a moment, then shrugged. "Tell them you don't want to talk. Call in sick. The whole thing will be settled by the time you come back."

He was still angry with her, but he was calm, eating his cheeseburger as though he was actually enjoying it. Her water boiled, but she turned off the burner and left it to sit.

"You're not worried?" she asked him, turning to face him again. "About your place in all this, I mean."

He smiled and didn't answer that. Which could mean he was confident, or that he'd resigned himself to humiliation. Who knew? She studied his chiseled face and realized she liked it an awful lot. More than she should.

"Michael," she said slowly. "What is the most important thing to you?"

He looked surprised at the question, then stopped and actually gave it some thought. "I guess being a vice president," he said at last. "It's been my only goal for a good long time.'' His hazel eyes met hers and he smiled rather sadly. ''After all, what else have I got in my life? I don't have a wife or two great kids to focus my time on. This is it for me.''

She bit her lip, distressed. That was one of the saddest things she'd ever heard.

But she quickly began thinking about her own situation. What was the most important thing to her? Her boys, of course. But once they were grown and gone? A little voice in her head asked the question. Then what?

She would take life as it came, raising her children the best way she knew how, sending them off, and then what would be would be. She could wait to find out about that one. All in good time.

''Michael,'' she said, watching him eat his cheeseburger as he leaned against the counter. ''Can I ask you one favor?''

He shrugged. ''No one's stopping you.''

She made a face at him, then got serious. ''When the board finds out who the women were who put out the calendar, could you please use your influence to keep them from being fired? If you can.''

He was staring at her and she couldn't read what he was thinking, but there was something going on in his eyes. Finally, he answered.

''If I have any standing left by the time this is all out in the open,'' he said softly, ''I'll do what I can.''

''Thank you.'' She smiled her relief.

But before she could say anything else, the telephone rang. Hannah had gone shopping and she didn't think there was anyone else around to answer it, so she did so herself. And for once, the call turned out to be for her. And of course, it was bad news. She listened to it, groaned, hung up and turned back to Michael.

"My house is trying to burn down," she told him tragically, throwing out her arms.

"What?" he asked, startled.

"Well, not really." She sighed. "But you know they are making a lot of renovations along with painting the interior. And there was an electrical fire in some of the new wiring in one of the walls, and there is some damage. It's going to put off our moving back home. Darn!"

"Was any of your property damaged?" he asked, looking sincerely concerned.

She sighed. "I'm not sure. I really should run over and take a look. But Hannah isn't here to watch the boys for me and..."

"I'll watch them," he offered, taking a last bite of his burger and gazing at her casually.

Her eyes widened. "You?"

He pretended to look over his shoulder. "Yeah, me. I don't see anyone else here."

She studied him suspiciously. "But you don't like children."

His dark look was appropriately exasperated.

"Maybe I don't like most children. But yours are okay."

Intrigued, she stared at him. "Really?"

"Yes, really." He glanced at the clock on the wall. "Look, I'll take them for a walk into town to get ice cream cones. How's that? By the time we get back, you should be done and back yourself."

It was a perfect plan. He did seem to have a knack for getting to the heart of an issue without too much flailing around. And for him to be so ready to help her when she'd turned down everything he'd asked of her lately...she was impressed with him.

"Thank you," she said simply, her eyes shining.

He shrugged. "No problem."

The board the next morning consisted of three grim-faced men and one woman, Mrs. Leghorn, who looked half asleep. Char and Michael sat facing them, waiting to be asked for their information while the members argued about another matter that seemed to have something to do with a lost golf ball holder. The longer they bickered, the more nervous Char got. She didn't like being in this position. The longer this took, the worse she felt about it.

She glanced sideways at Michael. He looked completely at ease, even letting a chuckle slip out when one member of the board made a particularly silly accusation about people switching golf balls on him when he wasn't looking. Michael didn't seem worried or angry or bothered in any way. Which annoyed her, for some reason.

Finally the board was ready to deal with the issue of the calendar. Mr. Strand plopped one of them on the table and turned to the page with Michael's picture. Holding it up for all to see, he turned and glared at Michael, but spoke to Char when he said, "I understand, Ms. Wolf, that you have information concerning the perpetrators of this monstrosity."

She lifted her chin and met their gazes calmly. "I'm sorry, sir," she said clearly. "I do not."

He stared at her. "Then why are you here?" he asked crossly.

"Good question," she responded, knowing she was skating on thin ice.

That started another squabble among the board members, one saying she shouldn't have been called, another saying she knew more than she was admitting and should be forced to tell all.

In the midst of the argument, Michael cleared his throat and rose to his feet.

"I'd like to say something about this, if I may," he said in a voice that stilled the others. "I understand your objections to finding my picture presented in rather poor taste in that calendar. But I didn't appear by choice. I didn't have any control over my picture appearing in it. It was definitely not something I sought." He paused, looking each one of them in the face in turn to emphasize his point. "Still, I think you are making much too much of this. It's just a silly joke. Now that you've stated your objections—and I've agreed with them, why don't we drop the matter?''

''Young man,'' Mr. Strand said, drawing himself up as though he wanted to make sure Michael knew he was important, ''do you understand what sort of people we want in our organization? You represent us. You are being given our most elite assignments and are being considered for one of the top positions in this company. This sort of shenanigan is unacceptable. Especially for someone who fancies himself a future vice president.''

Michael employed his most charming smile. ''I understand your objections and I endorse the sentiment. However, as I've stated, I think you're making a mountain out of a molehill.''

Mr. Strand stared belligerently and pointed to the calendar. ''Give me the names of the women who did this.''

''It happened on my first day here.'' Michael's smile only broadened. ''I don't know their names and hardly remember their faces.''

''We can show you pictures. You'll be able to identify them, I'm sure.''

''You could.'' He was still smiling. ''But I won't.''

Shock reverberated through the room as though they'd all been electrified. ''You won't?''

''I won't.''

Char gazed on in wonder. Somehow Michael

seemed the most mature person in the room, despite the far greater ages of the members of the board.

"I understand your outrage over this. I felt the same way at first. But then a friend set me straight, got me to look at the big picture. And I realized something. I'm not about to get someone fired over such an insignificant incident."

Char's heart was beating so fast, she thought she would faint. He meant her! He'd actually listened and he'd changed his mind because of her. She'd never been so thrilled.

But Mr. Strand looked as though he were ready to explode. On sudden impulse, Char jumped up to stand beside Michael.

"May I make a suggestion?" she said. "I think you should embrace this calendar."

"Oh, I do say," said another member of the board in exasperation.

But Char stood her ground. "I know you think I'm crazy, but consider this. The calendar is cute and funny. I think you should have an official version printed up, maybe with a disclaimer on the first page assuring everyone that it is all in good fun and not to be taken seriously. And you should distribute copies to the community."

They all gasped.

"Think about it," Char continued quickly. "We are a development company and development companies are getting a lot of flak these days. This could be the key to getting some good will in the community. It would show that we have a sense of humor and aren't the profit-grubbing old fogies people think we are."

"Young lady," Mr. Strand cried. "If this company didn't make a profit, you wouldn't have a job."

"I know that. And believe me, I love my job. I'm just talking public relations here."

The squabbling started up again. Mrs. Leghorn actually seemed to think Char had a good idea. Mr. Strand didn't agree. Michael looked down at Char and grinned. She smiled back and he took her hand. Seemingly forgotten by the bickering board, they walked out together.

"Do you think we'll both get fired?" she asked him as they made their way along the hall.

"What the hell?" he responded, squeezing her hand. "I can't think of anyone I would rather be fired with."

Her heart sang and she began to wonder if she would ever know a man she liked better than this one.

"Michael?" she said, looking up at him. "You wanted to talk to me about Ricky yesterday and I cut you off." She swallowed hard and looked up at him bravely. "It's hard to talk about those you love that way. But I think I'm ready now. If you still want to talk."

He raised her hand to his lips and kissed her fingers. "Not here," he said gruffly. "Can you get away for lunch?"

She nodded. "Meet you at noon," she said, and her heart began to race just thinking about it.

Le Café had private booths, which were just what they needed. Michael escorted Char to the most remote one he could find, nodding to the host who showed it to him and helping her into her side before sliding into his. They ordered and chatted quietly while waiting for the food to arrive. Once the waiter had finished with them, Michael took a deep breath, looked deep into her eyes and said, "Okay. Here goes."

Her heart was thumping for some reason. She could tell by his manner that he was going to tell her something he considered important, and that it was going to be difficult for him to do it. Was it about Ricky? Or himself? She wasn't sure and that set her on edge.

"I don't know much about kids. I haven't been around them since I was a kid myself. I'd pretty much convinced myself that I didn't want to be around them. But then I got to know your two and I realized...well, there's an exception to every rule, I guess."

He was saying he liked her boys. As a mother, that was surely a way to warm her heart. She smiled at him.

He didn't smile back. "Your boys are both great,

but I have to tell you, Char, as a friend...that I see something in Ricky that reminds me of myself as a kid. And I feel I have to alert you to...well, the fact that there may be a problem there.''

Her smile faded. She knew it would be easy to take offense again, but that wouldn't get her anywhere. So she steeled herself and nodded and waited for him to go on.

''I had some bad experiences as a child,'' he told her, his eyes darkening. ''My parents divorced and some other things happened. By the time I was ten or so, I was a very unhappy kid.''

He moved uncomfortably. ''You know, when you get wounded, your natural defenses form a scab over it, to let it heal. Well, sometimes I think you do that with your emotions, too. And when something hurts you as a kid, you don't know how to deal with it. So you cover it up and hope it will heal. And sometimes it does, and sometimes it doesn't. I pretty much put a mask over what was bothering me and hid it from the world. And when I look at Ricky, I think I can see him doing the same thing.''

He watched her eyes as he talked. She didn't want to hear this, and he couldn't blame her. No mother wanted to. But she was an adult. She should be able to handle it. Ricky was just a kid. He was the one who had to be protected. And he didn't really know what else he could say to convince her. How could he make her understand that he heard Ricky's cry for help the same way a dog can sense a whistle no one else can hear? He gazed at her, wondering what he could say to show her. And then she surprised him by reaching out and covering his hand with her own and looking deep into his eyes.

"What happened, Michael?" she said, her own eyes soft with sympathy. "When you were a child. What was it that hurt you so?"

And suddenly he found himself telling her—telling her things he'd never told anyone else. About how, once his parents divorced, he'd found that his father set up a schedule for visitation with his two younger boys, but not for him. Confused and terribly hurt, it took him years before he could fully understand his mother's explanation. For the first time, he learned that the man he'd considered his father was not his biological parent. He'd been almost three when his mother had married the man and then had two children with him. In the bitterness and acrimony of the divorce, the man was using Michael's parentage as a way to injure his mother, not seeming to care how he broke the heart of a young boy in the process. Every time Michael had to watch his little brothers prepare for an outing with their father and know that he wasn't invited, the knife dug more deeply into his heart.

He stopped talking when he saw the tears welling in her eyes.

"Hey." He gave her a crooked grin. "Don't cry about it. It hurt me, of course, but it also toughened me. Made me grow up. And then things didn't hurt me so much anymore.''

"Really?'' she said, her voice choked. "Or did you just learn not to let anyone see your pain?''

*Don't ever let them see you cry.* He stared at her. How did she know? Could she read his mind? *Don't ever let them see you cry.* That was the phrase he'd repeated over and over as a kid. Learn it, live it. That was the way it was.

He knew his childhood had messed him up in some ways, but he also knew he'd survived and he was doing okay, all in all. As a grown man, he could intellectualize the situation and know that his father had acted in illogical anger and used him to manipulate his mother. But still, the feeling had been planted deep inside him that there was something wrong with not being blood-related to a parent. Somehow that had made him not as good, not as worthy. And that had been the background of most of the problems in his marriage.

If he'd married a woman like Char…

But that was nuts. Grace had been a wonderful wife. He was the one who'd ruined that relationship, not Grace. If he'd been married to Char, it would have been the same old thing. The looks of disappointment would have been on Char's face. He winced, thinking of it.

"I don't want to wait until Ricky grows up to see if it comes out okay,'' she was saying. "Believe me,

Michael. I'm going to watch him carefully. And love him a lot."

He took a deep breath and let it out. "With a mother like you," he said warmly, "I think Ricky is going to be okay. And I probably shouldn't have said anything. But…"

"No." She put up a hand to stop him. "No, I'm glad you did. Sometimes I'm tempted to go along and ignore problems because they seem too scary to face. You made me stop and take note. That is a good thing."

"I just wanted to make sure you are aware…that you pay attention to make sure he doesn't get too close to the edge."

She nodded.

"And, Char, think about finding a good child therapist. It couldn't hurt."

She took his hand again, her eyes shimmering with unshed tears. "Michael, thank you. I know it wasn't easy to tell me all that stuff about your childhood. Thank you for making the effort and letting me into your life that way. I appreciate it."

Now he was getting embarrassed. "It's worth it if it helps you do something for Ricky."

Their gazes met and held. Something sparked between them, flaring like embers in a wildfire, and she dropped her hand quickly and put on a friendly smile as though it could protect her.

"There's something else you could do for me," she said lightly, playing with her salad fork.

"What's that?" he asked her.

"In case you hadn't noticed, it's Halloween." The office was plastered with decorations and she'd noticed that Lena was wearing a gypsy costume. There really wasn't any way he could have missed it.

"And that means?"

"Trick-or-treating. Tonight." She gave him an eager smile. "Want to help?"

He groaned. "I think I'll pass."

She arched an eyebrow and got tough about it. "I think not. You owe me."

"I owe you?" She was teasing, but he bit, anyway. "Why?"

"Didn't you know? Ronnie is going as you. I think that deserves some sort of recognition." She laughed at the look on his face. "Seriously, he's wearing a white shirt and dark slacks and a little tie. And I had to look all over, but I found him a little briefcase that he's going to carry."

He shook his head, wonder pouring through him. "You've got to be joking."

"Not at all." She smiled. "Ronnie is nuts about you, you know. You're his idol. So you be nice to my kid."

He was very nice to both her kids. They went out a little early, while it was still just barely light. Ronnie looked like a junior executive and Ricky was a wild little tiger. They were both excited, carrying their bags and walking up to the doors of the neighbors while Char and Michael stood back, watching.

"Trick or treat!" they called in unison.

And everyone opened their doors and laughed and told them how cute they looked and gave them candy or popcorn or a few coins.

"Look, Mama! Look! More candy," Ronnie would cry as he raced back to hug her around the knees and then ran on to the next house. Before long, she was carrying the little briefcase, as his hands were too busy with his ever-more-heavy sack of loot.

"I'm going to have to hide most of this candy after they go to sleep tonight," she told Michael conspiratorially. "And dole it out a little at a time."

"If there's any left after they pig out when we get home," he said cheerfully. "Odds are good you'll be down to the dregs." He grinned at her. "I remember Halloween. One of my favorite holidays."

He watched her laugh and he wanted to kiss her so badly, it stung inside. And suddenly he realized that he loved being here. He loved being with her and watching her kids. He almost felt as though he were a part of something. Almost.

Ronnie was, as usual, funny and fun to be with. And he'd even caught Ricky looking at him a few times. He looked away again very quickly when he realized he'd been spotted. But it was a beginning. And Michael was hopeful.

But most of all there was Char. She was so alive, so aware. And so damn sexy. He knew he should stay away from her. He knew they should never have gotten this close.

"Oh, well," he muttered to himself, watching her and enjoying the way the twilight colors played in her hair. "Too late now."

Too late. Too late to harden his heart to her appeal. Too late to keep himself from caring about her boys and what happened to them. Too late to keep from wishing there was some way he could have them all in his life for more than a temporary interlude.

# Chapter Eight

Char finally made contact with her uncle Zachary and he invited her to bring her brood up for a beach day on Saturday. She agreed happily. It had been so long since the boys had seen him and she wanted to make sure her little guys grew up with their great uncle as a part of their experience, as well as a part of their family. Besides, this would finally give her a chance to see if she could find out just exactly what was going on with his rebellion. She felt as though she owed it to Michael to at least make some sort of attempt. After all he'd done for her, she wanted to do something for him. If it was at all possible.

They piled into her old car with blankets and sand toys and implements of destruction and headed north. The day was gorgeous and her spirits were high.

She stopped off at the cliff site to show the boys where the main part of the resort would be built, and to her surprise, the place was swarming with workers. Cars, vans and trucks were parked haphazardly and a young woman in an orange jumpsuit was directing traffic.

She pulled her car up and let the boys out so that they could run in a sandy area for a few minutes. Shading her eyes against the sun, she looked around to see if there was anyone there that she knew, and was rewarded with quite a few appreciative glances and even a low whistle that took her aback.

"Hey, pretty lady," said Judd, the handsome construction worker, who spotted her right away. His gaze showed obvious approval of the way she filled out her designer jeans and blue jersey top. "We meet again."

"What are you all doing here?" she asked. "Don't you get weekends off?"

"Not this one. The powers that be made some plan changes and we've got to get the surveying done all over again by Monday. They've got ground-breaking next week. But we're happy. Overtime work means good pay."

His words were casual but his tone and attitude were definitely flirty, and she couldn't help but respond with a big smile. She was just about to say something equally inconsequential, just to keep the conversation going, when Michael suddenly appeared next to her.

"Hi," he said, glancing from Judd to Char and back to Judd again. Judd took the hint, winked at Char and got back to work. Michael looked at her sideways.

"There's another crew working over on the other side," he told her softly. "Maybe you'd like to walk over there and drive them crazy, too."

Char's mouth dropped in outrage. "Are you implying…?"

He held back a grin. "I'm not implying, I'm telling you. Construction guys like pretty women. And they're usually pretty noisy about it."

She calmed down, but she couldn't let him get away with that scot-free. "If you think I dropped by to get an ego boost, you can think again," she said, tossing her head. "We're on our way to have lunch with Uncle Zach and I thought I'd show the site to the boys while we were at it. I didn't know you all would be working today."

His gaze sharpened and he looked at her with a speculative frown. "Great idea," he said, as though she'd suggested something. "I'll come along with you."

"I didn't invite you," she protested, but her heart skipped at the thought of him coming along. That was happening more and more these days. Could she help it if she found him fun to be with? Despite everything, they got along very well.

Oh, who was she kidding? He was the sexiest thing to come along in her life for a good long time, and she responded to him like a flower to the sun. There were so many reasons why she shouldn't. To fall for Michael was to ask for heartbreak, not only for her but for her children as well. It wasn't fair to let them like him too much, to let them begin to see him as a father figure, when he had never pretended that he was going to be around any longer than his temporary assignment lasted. She wasn't about to follow through on the impulses his presence conjured up in her. But she wasn't about to banish him from her life, either.

"It's destiny, darling," he drawled, smiling at her. "Fate drew you here and threw me in your path. Don't try to fight it."

She couldn't help but smile back at him. She loved it when he was playful like this. "You've got nerve, haven't you?" she teased. "I feel so helpless. You're such a take-charge kind of guy."

"I'm glad you finally understand that," he responded smugly. "Hey, time's a wastin'. Let's go."

The boys came running up and Ronnie called out a greeting to Michael.

"Mr. Greco is going to go to Uncle Zach's with us," Char told them.

"Yeah!" Ronnie cried happily.

Michael grinned at him. "Hey. You want to ride with me?"

Ronnie nodded his head vigorously.

Michael looked at his brother. "How about you, Ricky?"

For the first time, there was a response in Ricky's eyes. For just a moment, he almost thought Ricky would agree to come along with him, too. But then he shook his head and came over to stand very close to his mother, twisting his hand in the hem of her shirt.

Looking up, Michael met Char's gaze, and for just a moment he felt a communication that didn't have words. Then she looked away and they both headed for their cars.

They had to take one of the car seats from Char's car and set it up in Michael's, which took some doing, but finally they were on their way. Michael looked in the rearview mirror at the happy boy in his back seat and he grinned. There was nothing like a smiling kid to put a glow on the day.

A little voice inside was yelling at him, asking him if he knew what the hell he was doing, but he was ignoring it. Yes, he'd promised to stay away from Char. And yes, he knew he was risking going through torture again. But right now, he didn't care. Being with Char was too good to give up just because he was going to have to pay a major price down the road. And that was all there was to it.

They pulled up alongside the little beach house moments later. The boys piled out, running into the yard and tackling Zach as he came out the door to meet them.

"Hey, you little rascals," he growled at them, laughing and hugging and then letting them run on into the house. Turning, he saw Michael and all humor drained from his face.

"Hey. This is a family party." Zach stared at Michael with unconcealed animosity. "I've said all I'm going to say to you and your damn company."

"He came with me, Uncle Zach," Char said, slipping her arm through Michael's. "He's my friend...and my boss."

Zach scowled, looking from her to Michael. "So you're still working for the bloodsuckers at Tri-TerraCorp, are you?" he said, his voice dripping with contempt.

"No rabble-rousing, Uncle Zach. Remember, this is a family party." She threw a significant glance toward the house, where the boys were playing, and leaned forward to kiss the old man's cheek.

Zach nodded, though he looked darn grumpy about it. He glared at Michael, but he stood back to let them both into his little house.

Zach's home was chock-full of mementos of the ocean. His wife had died fifteen years before, so there had been no one to inhibit his pack rat tendencies. From one end of the house to the other were items of seagoing lore that he'd collected over the years. Carvings of pelicans and seagulls sat shoved in between old life preservers, a huge clam shell, green glass fishing balls, a piece of a mast and half a rowboat. There was an old fishing net sitting in the corner and a sail tacked up on one wall. And everywhere there were seashells.

The boys were thrilled. They had to know what everything was and Zach lost most of his animosity toward Michael as he got into telling little anecdotes about each item. And once they'd exhausted that topic, the boys headed for the beach with shovels and pails in hand.

"Go on out and watch them," Zach said, shooing Michael and Char out the door as well. "And leave me to put the finishing touches on my secret chili recipe."

"Do you think I dare eat any food that old codger gives me?" Michael whispered as they went out through the front gate.

"Uncle Zach would never resort to poison," Char advised him. "I'd duck if he picks up a baseball bat, though."

"How reassuring."

She laughed. "Oh, come on. His bark is much worse than his bite. He's been gruff for as long as I've known him, and I've never seen him hurt a flea."

They walked out along the beach, the ocean breeze in their faces, the sun on their backs. Ronnie and Ricky were filling their pails with sand and storming down to the water's edge to throw their contents into the water, laughing with glee as the sand sank quickly out of sight.

"Are you going to try to talk to my uncle about clearing out of here?" she asked.

He shook his head. "No. I'm just here to judge the lay of the land, that's all. I'm not going to pick a fight."

"Good." She gave him a provocative smile. "You've made enough trouble for one day. Accusing me of soliciting construction worker whistles!" She rolled her eyes.

He gave her one of his adorable crooked grins. "I didn't mean it. You know that. I was just jealous."

Her eyes widened and she went very still. "Jealous? Jealous of what?"

He looked down at the sand, then looked into her eyes. "Of the way you were looking at Judd."

"I...." She flushed. "I can't believe you said that," she muttered, but her guilt was written all over her face. "I mean, it's not like we're... we're..."

"No, we're not, are we?" He caught hold of her hand and drew her closer. "And that's the only reason I'm not kissing you right now," he said softly.

She looked up into his luminous eyes and then away. She wanted his kiss so badly she could hardly breathe. But she couldn't let him. Not here. Not in front of the boys.

"I'll never be able to go to the beach again without thinking about how you looked dancing in the waves,'' he said softly, his eyes cloudy with the memory.

She turned to look at him, ready to make a bright, sassy retort, to say something, anything, to keep things light and casual, but the words died in her throat. Suddenly her eyes were swimming in tears. The unutterable sadness of what he'd said, the implication that they'd lost a chance at something that could never be retrieved, touched her in a way she hadn't expected.

"What's wrong?" he said when he noticed.

"Nothing." She wiped furiously at her eyes, appalled at herself. "It must be the sea air or something," she muttered transparently.

He curled her into the shelter of his arm and bent to plant a kiss on the top of her head. He didn't say anything, but he kept her there for the rest of their time on the beach, pressed close to his side, pressed close to his heart. And she reveled in the warmth of his body next to hers as the breeze tossed her hair.

The chili was wonderful, thick and spicy and covered with melted cheese. So were the light, fluffy biscuits Zach had made to go with it. They ate, laughing at silly things the boys said, listening as Zach regaled them with tales of "how it was in the old days."

It was obvious Zach had begun the stories as a way of sticking it to Michael, proving to him that he was a monster to be contemplating destroying what had once been so rich and special in this place. But as he got into it, he forgot all about that and his eyes became alive with the tales he was telling.

He told stories about sea captains washed ashore and nursed to health by Indian maidens, and of Spanish explorers staking out the land for Spain, and of settlers building their homes out of ships deserted by crews who jumped overboard to head for the gold fields, and of watching for enemy submarines during the Second World War. Then he told the boys things about their mother as a little girl, things that made them squeal with laughter and made Michael grin with delight—and Char blush.

They had little dishes of Zach's special banana chocolate ice cream, and then the boys wanted to go out and play again, and Char and Michael went out to watch them. They found some interesting hermit crabs living in a tidal pool in among the rocks. That kept them interested for half an hour, but while the two adults were still poking through trapped kelp, looking for beasties, the boys grew bored and were on the lookout for new horizons.

"Can we go on the pier?" Ronnie asked.

"Okay," Char said, glancing at it. It wasn't far from where they were wandering. "If you're very careful."

The boys ran off. She turned to Michael. "I suppose we'd better start back ourselves," she said. "It's about time to wrap up this little caper."

He agreed, but reluctantly. He was having one of

the better days of his life. Funny how they all seemed to revolve around Char lately.

He kept telling himself that he'd only come on this outing to check out Zach and maybe to try to ingratiate himself with the old man. But he knew better. He'd come because he had jumped at the chance to be with Char for an afternoon. He was beginning to think about her all the time. She filled his head, filled his senses, and if he wasn't careful, she would break his heart.

But silently, he scoffed at his own sappy thoughts. His heart had been broken years ago. What he carried around now was a shattered relic of what it might have been. He could be happy, he could be unhappy, but he couldn't be broken. Not anymore.

They started back, walking slowly, talking softly. As they neared the pier, Michael turned to take the shells they'd collected up to the house. Char watched him go, thinking warm and cuddly thoughts, but the sound of a large splash made her whip around. At the same time she heard Ronnie shout.

"Mama, Mama! Ricky fell in!"

"Oh, no!" She started for the pier, not terribly anxious at first. Both the boys took swimming lessons at the YMCA and Ricky had actually played in the water off that very pier only months before.

But Ronnie wasn't acting as though it were nothing. He was jumping up and down and pointing. "Mama, Mama, come quick. Ricky's going down."

That quickened her pace, and she began to panic when she saw the vague outline of Ricky's body going deeper into the water. And for a few seconds, she just couldn't understand it. She'd been taking the boys to swimming lessons since before they could walk. Ricky could swim. Why wasn't he moving? Why was he just floating away...?

"He hit his head, Mama. Right here." Ronnie pointed to his temple and jumped up and down with anxious excitement. "He hit his head on the wood. Quick, Mama. You gotta get him."

Before she could gather her wits and think what to do, something flashed past her and she realized it was Michael. In seconds, he was in the water, grabbing Ricky's body and pulling him to the surface.

"Ohmigod," she cried, running to the edge of the pier and helping to get Ricky up on the deck. He stirred, conscious now, and frowned as though he wasn't sure what had happened.

"Oh, my baby!" She pulled him into her arms. "Are you okay? Michael, is he okay?"

Instinctively she turned to him for reassurance. Sopping wet, Michael vaulted onto the deck and bent over the boy, checking his breathing, his pulse.

"He seems okay," he said roughly. "But I think a doctor should see him."

"I'll call an ambulance." Zachary had come out on the pier.

"Forget the ambulance," Michael said, lifting

Ricky into his arms and looking at Char. "Let's go. You drive my car. I'll hold him."

They did as he said, all four of them piling into Michael's car and racing for the hospital in downtown Trivolo. Char drove, forcing herself to remain calm and keep her mind on her driving. Ricky was still groggy, but he clung to Michael as though he knew exactly who had saved him from the water. The two of them were thoroughly wet, and she'd thrown a blanket over them before they'd left the beach. But she was numb, aware of what might have happened if Michael hadn't acted so quickly.

At the hospital, they all poured out and made their way into the lobby. A nurse hurried them on into the emergency room and a doctor was there to help in no time. Ricky was prodded and tested and given a red balloon. Michael and Ricky both were given dry clothes. And then there were more tests for Ricky.

"He's fine," the doctor said at last. "He had a bad bump, but I see no signs of concussion. No water in his lungs. Just a bad scare." He smiled at the boy. "But you had better be more careful on piers, young man. You might not always have such a quick lifeguard to save you as you did this time."

Ricky held tightly to his balloon, but he looked at Michael, who scooped him up to carry him to the car again. Char looked on in exhausted relief. Her boy was okay—thanks to Michael.

# Chapter Nine

Char sat in the semidark in the big overstuffed couch in the living room and cried her heart out. Her shoulders shook, her stomach ached, and her throat felt as though it had been burned. She'd been through more ups and downs in the last few weeks than she could handle without some kind of release, and tonight's episode with Ricky falling from the pier had been the icing on the cake. She had to let her emotions out and she couldn't do it where her children could hear her and get frightened. So she'd come downstairs in her robe and slippers after midnight and flung herself into the couch and wept, letting a torrent of anxiety and fear and regret and exhaustion pour out.

"Char?" Michael had come down to pick up some papers he'd left in the breakfast room and found her crying on the couch. He came to her immediately, dropping next to her and taking her into his arms. "Char! What is it? What's wrong?"

She looked up at him and smiled through her tears. "Oh, hi," she said, and then hiccuped. She blotted her face with the crumpled tissue she held in her hand. "Nothing's wrong."

"Don't tell me that," he said sternly. "I can see that something's wrong. What is it?"

"Oh." She took a deep breath and blinked a few times and smiled brightly at him. "Wow. That feels so much better."

He shook his head, bewildered. "What?"

"Having a good cry." She leaned her head back against his arm, enjoying the feel of him near her. Here she was in a state of semiundress again. She remembered the last time her near-naked body had pressed against his and suddenly she yearned to feel that way again. "I really needed one. Now I'm okay."

He looked at her in disbelief, his gaze taking in her tousled hair and the way her wet lashes clumped around her sparkling eyes. "You mean, you did this on purpose?"

"Cried?" She cocked her head to the side, considering. "Not exactly. Well, sort of. I've had so many competing emotions churning around inside, I had to get rid of them somehow." She blinked at him. "Oh, come on. You know what I mean. When men get upset, they yell and swear and break things. Women cry.''

He shook his head, but he was beginning to smile. ''You have a very simplistic view of human nature, don't you?''

She ignored what he'd said. Instead, she put the flat of her hand against his hard cheek and smiled at him. The room was rather dark, but she could make out his features very nicely, and she loved looking at his handsome face.

''Michael,'' she said softly, ''I just want to thank you for what you did today. And for being there.''

He covered her hand with his and said, ''That makes four hundred and eighteen.''

''Four hundred and eighteen what?''

''Times you've thanked me. Enough already. I've been overthanked at this point.'' His gaze skimmed over her pretty face and he dropped a light kiss on her lips. ''I'm going to get a swelled head. You won't be able to get rid of me.''

She laughed softly. That didn't seem like such a bad thing. Her lips tingled from where his had touched them. She wanted more, and knew she was playing with fire. Turning her head, she tried to force back the warmth that threatened to spread throughout her body. If only things were different and she was able to let herself go... A quick image of Michael naked and in her bed flashed in her mind, and she had to squeeze her eyes tightly to erase it again.

She knew she would have a hard time holding off a determined seduction, should Michael attempt one. And part of her was just a little disappointed that he didn't seem to sense her feelings at all. In fact, he seemed totally preoccupied by other considerations.

"I enjoyed seeing your uncle Zach today," he was saying. "And hearing his stories about the history of the beach area at Trivolo. I've got to admit it gave me a different perspective on things."

She looked back at him, pleased. "Did it? So you can understand why he clings to the place?"

"Oh, sure. I can understand that. Who wouldn't want to stay attached to such a great area, especially when he has a past there. But, time marches on."

"It does do that," she agreed softly.

He sighed. "Poor old guy." He tightened his arm and pulled her closer. She lifted her face toward his, but he was still talking. "You're lucky, you know," he said. "You've got that close happy family thing going with your uncle. I bet your parents are like that, too."

She sighed and lowered her face. He just wasn't paying attention tonight.

But then she nodded. "My parents are great, and I miss them now that they're living in Texas. But don't get the idea that everything is always rosy in our family. My father and Uncle Zach used to fight all the time. They even had a duel once." She giggled. "Or so they say. That was before I was adopted, though, so I can't vouch for it myself."

He went stock still, staring at her. "You're adopted?"

She nodded again. He stared at her with disbelief, drawing back so that he could see her better.

"You didn't tell me that. I can't believe it."

She made a face at him and snuggled down into her corner of the couch, pulling her robe in closer. "What's to believe? Adoption isn't freaky, you know. It happens all the time."

"But...I don't know." He waved a hand in the air. "You with this warm fuzzy family. I thought you were a prime example of why being blood-related is different."

That again. He really seemed fixated on his father's rejection. She moved so that she could face him more directly and tried to explain.

"It's not all that different from the regular way of being born into a family. I've never felt any different. In fact, when I was little, I was very proud that I was chosen to be a part of my family, not just some random leaving of the stork."

He was frowning in the shadows. "Char, you're assaulting all my theories of life. You don't feel damaged in any way?"

"Don't be silly. There wasn't a moment in time when I felt like they didn't love me as much because I was adopted."

He thought about that for a moment, then came up with a new question. "But what about your birth mother?"

"What about her?" She tossed her head. "I assume she was some young girl who wasn't married and couldn't handle having a child on her own. Thank God she did the smart and compassionate thing and found a good family to raise me. She gave me a wonderful childhood. I'll always be grateful to her."

"But, your birth parents are probably out there somewhere. Don't you ever want to know who they are?"

"Oh, sure, now and then I think about it and I'm curious. It would be interesting to find out something about them. Someday when I have lots of leisure time and nothing better to do, I might take a look. But it's certainly not a driving force in my life. It's no big deal." She smiled, trying to get a smile from him in return. "I have a mother and a father, you know. Most people are happy with one pair."

But he was frowning, genuinely disturbed by her revelations—and her attitude. "Why didn't you tell me about this when I told you about my childhood?"

"Michael." She took his hand, lightly stroking it with her own "You still don't get it. It's not something I think about all the time. I didn't even make the connection when you were talking about your father not being your birth father. Your childhood had nothing to do with mine. My childhood was perfectly happy. No one rejected me."

"How about your birth mother?"

"She didn't reject me. She honored me. She put my needs above hers. I can't think of a more unselfish thing to do."

He just sat there staring at her. It was very evident that he couldn't accept her explanation. She didn't know what else she could do to convince him. Maybe with time he would be able to digest her side of this and come to terms with it. But for now, she was tired of the subject. Finally she sighed and reached out and took his chin in her hand.

"Michael, my darling Michael," she said lovingly. "I've been sitting here dying to be kissed and all you want to do is talk about birth parents. If you're planning on any kissing at all, it's gotta be quick, because I'm heading back to my room and my kids in about thirty seconds."

"Kissing?" He looked down at her and then she could almost see one door closing in his mind and another opening. He pushed away the concerns about his own childhood and welcomed her in as he gathered her up in his arms. "I'll show you kissing, lady," he told her huskily.

She sighed with contentment as his mouth settled over hers, opening to his approach with the eagerness that parched earth might meet a summer rainfall. He felt so warm and strong and he smelled like soap and sunshine. She sank into his embrace and responded, losing her mind to the more compelling thrust of sensuality. She was all heat and moisture and sliding sensation, and when she felt his hand slip in and cup her naked breast, her nipple responded as though it might burst with rapture, and the quiver of hot desire spread quickly through her body and centered with aching hunger right where she needed him most.

"Oh!" she cried, pulling away. "Oh, Michael, I…"

He pulled her back and kissed her hard, then drew away himself.

"Better go up to your kids," he told her huskily. "You stay here one more minute and I can't promise you gentlemanly behavior."

She laughed softly as she pulled her clothes together and rose from the couch. "Good night," she told him ruefully as she quickly left the room.

"'Night," he echoed behind her.

Once upstairs, she stopped and closed her eyes for a moment before opening the door to where her children slept. She pictured Michael in her bed, his arms wrapped around her, his body shining gold in the lamplight, and she gasped aloud.

"Oh, I want him so," she whispered to herself. But with a deep, deep sigh of regret, she went into her room and closed the door against him, and against her thoughts of lovemaking. Once inside, she was all mother. The lover in her stayed out in the hall, languishing from lack of attention, crumbling slowly into dust. And that was just the way it had to be.

But she knew that something had changed. Michael was like a part of her now. Wherever she went, whatever she did, he was in the back of her mind, at the edges of her consciousness, always there. And how long could that go on without her doing something about it?

The next two weeks passed very quickly. The ground-breaking on the cliff-top section of the White Stones Resort had begun. They'd left the beach section out as full title wasn't settled yet. Char knew Michael wanted her to go talk to her uncle, and after all he'd done for her—after all he now was to her—she was determined to do it, no matter how hard it might be.

The only problem was, she could never get in touch with Zach. He wasn't answering his telephone. She'd been by the place twice, leaving notes on the door that didn't get a response. She could tell that someone was still living in his house. It had that look, as though someone had been there in the last few hours and would be coming back any minute. So she had no fear of foul play. Still, where was he?

On her second trip to the beach, she'd found one of the neighbors filling his car with household items and she'd asked where her uncle might be. But the neighbor just mumbled something about how he was giving up the fight.

"Zach doesn't talk to me anymore," he told her resentfully. "He thinks I'm a traitor."

She called Annie May at her daughter's house,

but her old friend hadn't seen her uncle since the last time she'd been by her old house. "Have you tried the senior center?" she suggested. "I know he used to go there every Wednesday for pinochle."

She tried, to no avail. No one at the center had seen him for weeks. She supposed she could camp out on his doorstep and wait for him to show up, but she didn't have the time, what with her job, the kids—and then there was Michael.

Michael had been wonderful. He'd joined her and the boys in doing something almost every day. Whether it was going for pizza, riding the little train at the petting zoo, playing miniature golf or eating frozen bananas on the boardwalk, everything was more fun when Michael was involved. She knew the boys were getting seriously attached to him and she knew it wasn't wise to let them do that with a man who wasn't going to be around after a few months, but it was too late to stop it now. Extreme bonding had already taken place. She and her kids were in this for the entire ride and all they could do was hold on tight and hope for the best.

She had no idea how much longer he would be staying. The project was moving along briskly and he was considered a genius by some for the excellent work he'd done at Trivolo. All except for the beach strip, but there seemed to be some patience regarding the holdouts, at least from the powers in the organization. Gillette Johnson was known to be pushing that as a major flaw. It didn't seem to be getting a lot of leverage at this point, but if things weren't finalized soon, he might have an issue on his side.

The interesting thing was, the board had more or less taken up Char's idea about the calendar, though Sherry's wasn't the version they had decided to put out. That would have been a little too much. But they were putting together one with pictures of various workers at TriTerraCorp doing their jobs, with funny sayings and cute words of wisdom. They planned to distribute them all over Trivolo and Rio de Oro. Early word-of-mouth was quite enthusiastic.

"You know," she'd said when a couple of the board members had called her in to take a look at how her idea was being implemented, "what we ought to do is have an open house and let people of the community come through and see what we really do here. We could have clowns and popcorn machines and balloons for the kids...."

Mrs. Leghorn, the only female member of the board, looked thunderstruck. "What a wonderful idea," she said. "I'll look into feasibility studies right away."

And the next thing Char knew, she had a promotion and a pay raise—and a personal invitation to lunch from Mrs. Leghorn, who wanted to know what other ideas she might have up her sleeve.

"There you go," Michael said when he congratulated her. "You're on your way. You'll be chairman of the board before we know what's hit us."

"Why not?" She laughed and pretended to toss her hat in the air. "The sky's the limit."

"You're the limit," he said, and he kissed her. It was a quick kiss, a glancing blow.

They had been doing a lot of kissing lately, but they'd all been like that. Just little kisses, light and friendly. Nothing deep or passionate since the night on the couch. But she knew from the look in his eyes that there was plenty of passion smoldering inside him—and she knew from the way her heart raced when he was near—that a certain passion was smoldering deep within her as well. And that was why she had to stay on her toes and keep strict control.

Meanwhile, she was getting ready to move back into her house. Work had been completed and she was just waiting for the final cleanup before she piled her kids into her car and headed for home. She'd been by the house a couple of times on her own, just to tidy up and prepare for the big return. And while there, she'd found one of her old pictures of Danny.

Looking at it, she couldn't imagine why she'd ever thought Michael looked a thing like him. He was totally different. She studied the wild, rebellious look on Danny's face. It was a look that had thrilled her when she was younger. Now he just looked callow and immature. In contrast, everything about Michael was what she wanted in a man.

Was she in love?

''Am I ever!'' she whispered ruefully.

And then she moaned and put her head into her hands. What in the world was she going to do about it? She was in love with a man who didn't want to marry anyone. Well, she'd been there before and she couldn't let the same thing happen again. But was there any way to convince Michael to take another look at the marriage game?

When she'd first known him, his rationale had been that he didn't want to be around children. She'd understood that. And if that was the way it was, she couldn't be around him.

But things had worked out very differently from what they'd both expected. He'd lost his distaste for children and now he adored the boys. And they more than adored him. Ronnie had from the beginning; but ever since the incident at the pier, where Michael had saved him, Ricky had become his biggest fan, too. They got along great. There was no reason for him to say he couldn't be around kids any longer.

So what was it that was holding him back? Was it his first marriage? He'd never really explained what had happened there. She didn't know if that was it, but she knew darn well there was something. She did know that he felt that what he'd gone through in his childhood had somehow made him incapable of being a good husband and father. But she didn't believe that. Even if you couldn't totally get over these things, once you dealt with them hon-

estly you could build your life around them. She was
going to have to talk to him and try to find out just
what was going on in his head and heart. She wasn't
looking forward to it. But this thing needed to be
dealt with.

But then her brave front crumbled. Oh, how could
she try to fool herself this way? She knew darn well
talking wasn't the answer. You couldn't talk someone into committing to you if their heart wasn't in
it.

So...what now? Just go on as she was and get
ready for the heartbreak—and hope that time would
change things.

But suddenly there was no more time.

"I'm being sent back to Florida," Michael said a
few days later as he walked into the kitchen where
she was fixing hot dogs for her boys' dinner.

She whirled and stared at him, the mustard bottle
still in her hand. Her heart plummeted and she felt
dizzy for a moment.

"Why?"

He gazed at her, his eyes guarded, but still revealing a discomfort with this news that couldn't
help but reassure her, just a little. "Because they
think they've got the White Stones project under
control out here and another project is falling apart
back there. Purchasing agreements are coming un-
raveled. They need me to clean up the mess."

Of course they needed him. From what she could

gather, he was the best. The vice presidency was all but in the bag.

"But you'll be coming back?" she asked, trying not to sound as anxious as she felt.

"I think so." He ran a hand through his hair, making it stand up almost as high as Ronnie's. "But I can't be sure and I don't know when."

She went back to fixing hot dogs, but her mind was racing. She'd known he would be leaving at some point, but she'd thought it would be much further in the future. A knot of dread formed in her stomach. They were going to lose him. Suddenly she was very much afraid that her fears were justified. What were her boys going to do without him?

Michael filled her in on the details. They had only a little over twenty-four hours left. They had to fill it with something special.

"What can we do?" she asked quietly a few minutes later, watching her boys eat their hot dogs and feeling as though there had been a death in the family. Twenty-four hours. And sometime in that space she was going to have to ask him if he'd changed his mind about marrying, or if he was planning to walk away with barely a backward glance. It had to be explored. She had to do it, if he didn't.

"I know," he said, brushing her silvery hair back off her cheek and smiling at her. "Take the day off, take the kids out of day-care. Let's go to Disneyland."

"Really?"

"Have they ever been?"

"No." She glanced over to make sure they hadn't heard what he was saying.

"Great." He looked at them, too. "I want to be the one to take them the first time."

She sighed, looking at him and wondering how he could not feel the love she sent his way every minute of the day. "They will be so excited."

Early the next morning they were off for Disneyland. The drive down took more than two hours but there wasn't much traffic on the freeways and they arrived just before the park opened. It was a beautiful day with small white clouds scudding at the edge of a bright blue sky and a cool breeze blowing. The place was remarkably uncrowded on this mid-November day. They hopped on one ride after another with barely a wait. The boys were in heaven, especially when two character actors dressed as Mickey and Minnie Mouse stopped to pat their heads and posed for pictures with them. Later they ate some fast food and then took the boys to Tom Sawyer's Island, where they could run through the caves while Char and Michael sat on a rock looking out over the water and watching the river boat go by.

*Now,* thought Char. *I should bring it up now.*

But what was she going to say? "Hey, have you gotten over that phobia about marriage yet?" That might work. Except that she didn't know if she could say it in a tone that didn't put his back up.

Or maybe, "I love you, Michael. I don't want to lose you this way."

No, she knew she couldn't say that without tearing up and she would die before she cried over him—at least, right in front of him.

He put an arm around her and drew her close. "I wish this was nighttime with stars in the sky," he whispered in her ear. "Then we could sit here and make out for hours."

"I'd like to make out for hours with you sometime," she said, looking just a bit plaintive.

"You picked a fine time to tell me that," he said, nuzzling into her neck. "I'm leaving in the morning."

Turning her face, she kissed him. The kisses were quick but hungry. Couldn't he feel her need for him in her kisses? Or was she just fooling herself to think he might care?

"I wish you weren't going," she said, and she just barely kept her voice from trembling.

He didn't say anything, but he held her close and buried his face in her hair.

They gathered the boys and took the raft off the island, then walked down Main Street, looking at the sights. And then they were in the car, driving home with two little sleepyheads nodding in the back.

"What a lovely day," she said.

He nodded. But he didn't talk all the rest of the way home and she sat, wondering why she was such a coward, why she couldn't bring up the questions she wanted answered most.

It was getting late. Char had finally put the boys in their beds and she was down in the kitchen, getting herself a last drink of water before going to bed herself.

Oh, to heck with it, she thought to herself as she half listened to Hannah chattering away about her son in Vancouver while she gave the kitchen a last evening tidy. Don't try to kid yourself. You came down in hopes of seeing Michael one last time tonight. Didn't you?

And suddenly, there he was. Their eyes met and they both smiled, both knowing darn well what was going on. But Michael went to the refrigerator and got out the milk, pouring himself a tall glass and giving Hannah the correct answers when she paused for breath. At the same time, he was stealing glances at Char.

Finally, Hannah went to see if the front door was locked, and he leaned close and whispered in Char's ear, letting his fingers trail seductively down her neck.

"Come to me tonight, Char. When everyone is in bed. It's our last chance."

Before she could answer him, Hannah was back. "Well, good night, you two," she said cheerfully. "I'm off. See you first thing in the morning."

"'Night," they echoed in unison. And as soon as

her footsteps had faded on the floorboards, Michael turned to Char again.

"Well?" His eyes were luminous.

She shook her head, though her heart was thumping in her chest. "Oh, Michael. I can't."

"Yes, you can." He touched her cheek. "You know you want to."

She shook her head sadly. "Whether I want to or not, I'm not doing that again without a ring on my finger," she said firmly.

His gaze darkened along with his handsome face. "I can't marry you," he said bluntly.

"Really?" She felt as though she'd been slugged in the stomach. Here was the answer to her question, only it certainly wasn't the answer she'd been hoping for. But his attitude, the way he'd put it, just made her angry. "Why not? I'd say we were pretty well suited in a lot of ways."

"We are." He turned toward the window. "In every way except one."

"What are you talking about?" she said, following him and leaning against the counter beside him.

He ran a hand through his dark hair and stared out into the night. "You want more children. I've heard you say so."

She stared at him for a moment, then frowned. "I thought maybe you were over that kid phobia thing."

He shook his head. "It's not that. Actually, it was never that."

"Then what?"

His face was hard as granite as he turned to look into her eyes. "Char, I can't have children. I've taken tests and the results are conclusive. I'm sterile." A flash of pain showed in his eyes, then died away. "And don't tell me it doesn't matter. It matters. I've lived it mattering. That's what broke up my marriage. That's what keeps me from making a commitment to any other woman. I know it would come between us eventually."

She shook her head, trying to assimilate all he was saying and put it into perspective. "Do you mean to tell me your wife left you because you're sterile?"

He hesitated. "No. She left because I couldn't deal with the fact that I was sterile. There's a difference." He obviously thought that was enough, but when she shook her head in bewilderment, he went on. "You know my experience with my so-called father made a mess of me for a while. I mostly got over that." He paused, having difficulty explaining fully. "But somehow I couldn't get over the feeling that I wasn't good enough for him because I wasn't blood-related." He searched her eyes, looking for a hint as to whether she understood at all. "So when Grace wanted to adopt... I just couldn't do it." He shrugged. "She wanted a family. She went to find one."

"You couldn't adopt a child? Because of that insane blood-related thing you keep going on about?"

''That's about it. I can't help but feel that there's a difference there.''

He stared at her and she didn't know what to say. His head went back as though he had decided she just didn't care, and she grabbed his arm to make him stay and listen.

''You know what?'' she demanded. ''You're crazy. Do you think for one minute that I would give you up just because I couldn't have more children with you?''

''Char, I've been through this. I already know how it comes out.''

Her eyes narrowed. She was furious with him. ''This has got to be about more than that,'' she said accusingly. ''You've got it in your head that you could never love my boys because you're not their birth father. That you could never be a real father to them. That's what you're telling me, isn't it?''

He hesitated and finally said, as though it pained him, ''I don't know if I could or not.''

She shook her head, angry with him, angry with herself for loving him. ''All I know is—if you don't think you can, you can't. And if you can't—then there's no point in going on with this conversation.''

He winced. ''Just like that.''

Her eyes flashed. ''Just like that.''

He shrugged, looking angry as well. ''I guess this is goodbye, then.''

She nodded. ''Goodbye, Michael. I'm sorry you are so determined not to be happy.''

He didn't say another thing. She raced back to her room and paced the floor for ten minutes, her mind furiously going from one thing he'd said to another. She'd never been so angry.

Finally, she couldn't stand it. Slipping out of her room, she knocked softly on his door. He was there in an instant, letting her in. She could see by the look in his eyes that he thought she'd come to him the way he'd first hoped—and that only made her more angry with him.

"I have something else I have to say to you," she said evenly as he closed the door again. "And don't you think for one moment I've come here to tell you all is well, because I haven't."

He crossed his arms over his bare chest and stared at her. He looked like a Greek statue, only he still had his pants on. Angry as she was, she felt breathless at the sight of him.

"Then what are you here for?" he demanded.

She raised her head and glared at him. "I just have one thing to say to you. If you think that anyone cares about you being sterile—anyone besides yourself, I mean—then you are a bigger fool than any I've ever met. The only person in this world who cares about it is you."

He was shaking his head as though he thought she was nuts, but she didn't give him time to say anything. "You know what I think? I think you've used your sterility as a shield. I think you use it to keep others at bay, so you don't have to get involved and make a commitment.''

He reached for her. ''Char...''

''No, you wait,'' she said, stepping back out of his reach. ''I don't care if you're sterile. It makes not one whit of difference to me. But I do care that you think it would make a difference. In other words, you don't think much of me, do you? And that's all I've got to say to you.''

She reached out and opened the door and left, half thinking he might come after her. But he didn't. And she went into her room and threw herself down on her bed and cried herself to sleep, making very sure to do it quietly so that her children wouldn't hear her.

# *Chapter Ten*

Char spent the next few days going over all the things she should have said in her head. Why hadn't she waited, why hadn't she said, "Let's talk it over in the morning," when she could have dealt with it rationally instead of in a rage? Why hadn't she made him look at the inconsistencies in his emotional reactions? Why hadn't she been a bit more understanding?

But most of all, why hadn't she told him that she loved him?

It might have made a difference. Now she would never know. Because he was gone.

She and the boys said goodbye to the old Victorian a few days later, moving back into their house. Their neighbors were so glad to have them back—and to have the construction noise gone—they threw them a little party. It was a lot of fun to see friends they'd been missing for the last couple of months.

But what wasn't fun was every evening when the boys looked at her with puzzled eyes and asked, "Where is Mr. Gecko?"

Ronnie said, over and over, his eyes huge with worry, "Mama, he's *gotta* come see our house."

And Ricky, who had grown especially close to Michael in his quiet way, said, "I'm saving my jelly beans from Dizzylan' for him."

Ricky was especially worried when he didn't show up, but Ronnie missed him, too. They didn't seem to understand her explanation that he had gone to Florida. One evening when the name of that state was mentioned on television, they both raced to sit in front of the screen, hoping to see the man they both missed like crazy.

She'd been calling around, getting recommendations for therapists. She wanted Ricky evaluated, but what she contemplated was a family appointment, so that the therapist could watch all three of them interact and make judgments based on real-time observation. Then she could get advice on whether or not she was blowing this whole thing out of proportion.

She missed Michael terribly. And there was one thing she could still do for him. By hook or by crook, she was determined to do what he'd wanted weeks ago—go to her uncle and convince him to give up his fight and make way for the White Stones project.

Putting a little new steel in her spine, she girded her resolve and headed for the beach one blustery afternoon. For once, she found him at home. But, to her surprise, he was packing up all his things.

"What are you doing?" she demanded. "Are you giving up the fight?"

"The fight?" He looked at her as though she'd gone stark raving mad. "What fight?"

"Uncle Zach, you know very well what fight!"

"Oh, you must be talking about my little rebellion against the big bad corporation."

"Yes, that fight."

"Ach, that's in the past. Here, hand me that oar. I think I'll pack it in with the mast."

"Uncle Zach, come on. Come clean."

"There's nothing much to tell. I worked things out with your Michael Greco." He shook a finger at her. "That's one smart cookie you've got there. You better hang on to that boy. He's going places."

"He's going places, all right. In fact, he's gone."

"Gone? Gone where?"

"To Florida."

"Sorry to hear that. Maybe you should take a little trip, huh?"

She threw out her hands, exasperated with him. "Uncle Zach, tell me what happened."

"We made a deal, Michael and I. It was mostly my doing, of course. You know, people have always said I have a great gift for storytelling. And I think I proved it the other day. In fact, I convinced that fellow of yours that the history of this area is precious enough that we oughta not lose it.''

"Really?" She watched him talk, stunned but growing ever more pleased with what he was telling her.

"Michael decided, if I were to sign over my property, he would pledge to use this part of it as a museum, a place where we'll keep a record of all the peoples and animals that have come through here over the years, from saber-toothed tigers to missionaries to high tech. It'll be a centerpiece to the resort, give it a theme to decorate around and all that. And I'm going to be curator."

"You're kidding!"

"Well, we'll have a professional curator, of course. But I'm going to be the consultant. That's where I've been lately—meeting with people, getting plans in place. I even spent some time in L.A." He made a face. "So, you think it's a good idea?"

"I think it's a wonderful idea."

"Yeah, that Michael Greco. Like I say, you'd better hang on to that guy."

If only she could.

But she got a commitment from Zach to join them for Thanksgiving. She wasn't really looking forward to it, and at the same time, she was telling herself she was being silly. It wasn't like Michael had ever been with them on the holiday before. So why was she feeling as though it wasn't going to be a very thankful day without him?

"Pure self-indulgent self-pity," she told herself contemptuously. But that didn't stop her.

Michael was lonely. It was the first time since he was a boy that he'd felt this alone. When Grace had left him, there had been enough anger and resentment to keep him warm at night. But now he didn't have much of anything.

He'd been angry with Char over the things she'd said to him at first. But the more he thought her accusations over, the more he thought she'd seen right through him into some kind of truth that he'd never faced before. Funny. Had he used his sterility as a shield? In some ways, he imagined he had. It had almost become a sort of secret excuse to use when things didn't go well. She was right. It was time to ditch it. He would have to think about that when he had more time.

He was working hard. The project was going well, though he was working every hour of his waking day to get things back in shape. The sooner he finished up, the sooner he might be assigned back to the West Coast. So far there hadn't been a word on when he might be allowed to return.

And that brought up another question. Did he really want to go back? There was an easy answer. He was dying to.

He did take one break when a co-worker, Barney

Higgs, invited him along to SeaPark one Sunday. By this time he'd realized he could probably use some kind of break to freshen his attitude. It was interesting seeing all the different fish and the killer whales and the dolphin shows.

The dolphins were the most intriguing, in his opinion. The pretty young girl in a skimpy outfit giving them a running commentary on what was going on in the larger tank told them something that made him think.

"Here is Freddy, our new little baby dolphin," she said into her microphone. "Freddy's mother died shortly after giving birth to him, which was very sad, but Freddy was immediately adopted by Gigi, who had just given birth about a month before. Their little family is so tight, we don't think either of them remembers it was ever any other way."

"That often happens with animals in the wild," Barney said to Michael as they strolled on to the next exhibit. "The mother gets killed and the baby animal gets adopted by another one of the herd or whatever. Sometimes even by an animal of another species. Just like humans." He laughed. "We're all basically animals, I guess."

He didn't think much about it at the time, but that image of the baby dolphin stayed with him over the next few days, and he kept thinking about how easily the other dolphin had taken over the mothering.

It was finally dawning on him. He was the one who was out of step. He was the one who just didn't get it. He couldn't love Char's boys any more if they were his flesh and blood. The whole animal kingdom was wiser than he was.

"What the hell's the matter with me?" he muttered, staring at his reflection in the hotel room mirror. "What...have I been crazy all these years?"

"Yes," the mirror said back. "Crazy and self-destructive and risking ruining your own life."

"You're right," he said into it. "I've got paradise waiting for me out on the West Coast and here I am in Florida talking to a mirror."

Still, what was he going to do about it? Work hard, he supposed, and see what happened.

The next day, he took a phone call from the Rio de Oro branch, as he often did, but this time, Char was on the line.

"Michael, is that you?"

"Yes," he said. "Hi." The sound of her voice was curling his hair.

"Hi," she said back. "I'm sending you a report that needs some signatures. Is that okay?"

"Oh, sure." He just wanted her to keep on talking. If he closed his eyes, he could see her pretty mouth as he heard her sexy voice.

"How are things?" she was saying.

"Oh, fine. Everything's coming along pretty well."

"I saw Uncle Zach. I know all about the deal you made with him."

"Oh, that's come through, has it?"

"Looks like."

"Good." The voice was so wonderful. He almost felt as though he could reach out and touch her. "And the boys?"

She hesitated. "Oh, they're fine."

Suddenly he saw them as well. "Do they miss me?" he asked, his voice just a little husky.

When she didn't talk for a moment, his fingers tightened on the receiver.

"Char? Are you still there?"

"Yes." She was obviously trying very hard to make her voice sound normal. "Yes, of course the boys miss you."

Her voice was trembling and he began to worry. "Char, what's wrong?"

"Nothing."

"Char. Something's wrong. What happened?"

"Nothing." She started to laugh softly. Or was that crying? He couldn't be sure. "Nothing at all. Except that we all miss you." Her voice broke and she said quickly, "I have to go now. Bye."

"Char!"

But she was gone.

Just hearing that voice again tied his stomach in knots. This was insane. He had to get out of here. He had to get back to where it had seemed his life was worth living.

Char hung up and groaned, wiping her eyes. She couldn't stand the thought of being one of those women who wept on the phone and begged men to come back to them. The phone rang, and for a moment, she considered ignoring it. But finally, she picked up the receiver.

"Chareen Wolf here."

"Char? I'm coming back."

It was Michael. Her heart leaped and she gasped.

"You're coming back. For sure?"

"Yes. Right away." There was a pause, then he added, "Do you want me to?"

"Yes. Oh, yes." Tears were pouring from her eyes. She was just too emotional to keep things under control as she usually did.

"Are you crying?" he demanded.

"No," she lied shakily.

"You're crying," he said accusingly.

"No, ignore that," she told him. "I want to know why...how you're coming back. Is the project finished back there?"

"I've got it on track. They can handle it. But I'm getting out of here. I've got to come see you and the boys."

"You mean, you're just coming on your own? Without the company's blessing?"

"That's right. If they don't like it, they can fire me."

She didn't know what to say. This was so unexpected. "But Michael, what if they do?"

"Then I'll get another job. Hell, I'll go fishing with Zach every day if it comes to that." His voice was warm, loving, just the way she liked to remember him best. "You just get ready, because I'm going to be there within the week."

"I'll be ready."

"Good."

She hung up and stood in the middle of the office, quivering. What did it mean? She couldn't be sure. But she would be ready. Oh, boy, would she be ready!

She heard he was back at three in the afternoon on Friday, and she started running. She ran down the third-floor hallway, glanced at the open elevator and ignored it for the stairs, which she took two steps at a time, to the fourth floor, then ran down that hallway straight into his office. She didn't stop to say anything to Lena. She didn't ask if he was free. She just burst right into his office and flew right into his arms.

"Michael!" she cried, showering his beloved face with kisses. "Oh, Michael! Do you love me?"

"Yes," he said readily, holding her tightly in his arms and looking a bit bemused. "I love you."

"Great." Her face was shining with relief. "Then, will you please marry me? Because I want to make love with you as soon as possible."

"Miss Wolf, please" came a voice from right behind her. "This is a place where business is transacted, not a singles bar."

She dropped from Michael's arms and whirled to find Mrs. Leghorn frowning at her over her glasses.

"Oh," she said, flushing. "I didn't... I mean..."

"You are interrupting a very important meeting," Mrs. Leghorn continued as though she hadn't spoken at all. "Mr. Greco was attempting to explain this extraordinary behavior. He is supposed to be in Florida. He is not supposed to be here."

"And I am trying to explain to Mrs. Leghorn," Michael said, "that I am no longer interested in answering to the board as to what I am 'supposed' to be doing."

Mrs. Leghorn rolled her eyes. "Cut the melodramatics," she said crisply. "We know very well why you came back. Everyone knows everything in this company. Don't try to pull the wool over our eyes."

Michael glanced at Char and grinned. "They know it all," he told her, shrugging.

"Everything?" She looked at Mrs. Leghorn and smiled, feeling impossibly happy and not sure if she deserved to just yet.

Mrs. Leghorn made a disapproving moue and went on. "You do know that plans are afoot to have you installed as the new vice president next week."

Michael shrugged again, looking unconcerned. "Plans can change," he said carelessly.

Her gaze sharpened. "Are you telling me you aren't interested?"

"Well, that depends. Does the job mean I'll be out here in California?"

Mrs. Leghorn sighed as though she were being indulgent to an unruly teenager. "That's part of the bargain, of course. We've taken your preferences into account." As an aside to Char, she said, "This new breed of executive. So pushy and spoiled." Turning back to Michael, she added, "We think we can live with it." She looked at him expectantly. "What say you?"

Michael grinned at Char. "I say, sounds pretty good. But the whole thing is conditional on whether or not Ms. Wolf will marry me."

Char beamed at him. "Ms. Wolf ecstatically accepts the proposal, Mr. Greco," she said.

His smile caressed her as surely as his hands might, and then he looked up at the older woman. "Then I guess, Mrs. Leghorn, we've got a deal."

Mrs. Leghorn sighed with seeming relief. "Good." She smiled at them both. "Well then. Let the merger begin."

Michael's face registered shock. "Mrs. Leghorn!"

She waved at him indulgently. "Oh, kiss the darn bride, would you? I'll retreat to ready the paperwork." And she made her way imperiously out of the office, closing the door behind her.

Michael turned to Char and drew her back into his arms. "Let me hold you," he said softly, pulling her tightly against his long body. "Oh, my love, I've missed you so much."

"Me, too. I love you so much, Michael," she murmured, closing her eyes and savoring the joy she felt. It was really going to happen. She was going to marry the man of her dreams. But one last thing nagged at her.

"Michael?" she said, drawing back. "The boys…"

"How long do you think we should wait before telling them to call me Dad?" he asked her.

"About two seconds," she said with pure contentment, and finally her world was complete.

\*    \*    \*    \*    \*

*In February 2002, look for*

SHE'S HAVING MY BABY!

*By Raye Morgan,*
*part of Silhouette Romance's*
*heartwarming new continuity series,*

HAVING THE BOSS'S BABY.

SOME MEN ARE BORN TO BE ROYALTY.
OTHERS ARE MADE...

# CROWNED HEARTS

A royal anthology featuring,
NIGHT OF LOVE, a classic novel from
international bestselling author

# DIANA PALMER

Plus a brand-new story in the MacAllister family series by

## JOAN ELLIOT PICKART

and a brand-new story by

## LINDA TURNER,

which features the royal family of the upcoming
ROMANCING THE CROWN series!

*Available December 2001 at your favorite retail outlet.*

*Where love comes alive*™

Visit Silhouette at www.eHarlequin.com
PSCH

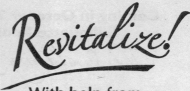

Celebrate the season with

*Midnight Clear*

A holiday anthology featuring
a classic Christmas story from
*New York Times* bestselling author

# Debbie Macomber

Plus a brand-new *Morgan's Mercenaries* story
from *USA Today* bestselling author

# Lindsay McKenna

And a brand-new *Twins on the Doorstep* story
from national bestselling author

# Stella Bagwell

*Available at your favorite retail outlets in November 2001!*

*Silhouette*®
*Where love comes alive*™

Visit Silhouette at www.eHarlequin.com        PSMC